M000119911

BROKEN LEAVES

RICHARD
M PEARSON

This is a work of fiction. Names, characters, places, and incidents either are the product of the author's imagination or are used fictitiously. Any resemblance to actual persons, living or dead, events, or locales is entirely coincidental.

Copyright © Richard M Pearson 2019

All rights reserved. No part of this book may be reproduced or used in any manner without written permission of the copyright owner except for the use of quotations in a book review.

First Edition

Cover design & Typesetting by Ryan Ashcroft
BookBrand.co.uk

All rights reserved

'Broken Leaves' is the third novel by Richard M Pearson.

I released my first book 'The Path' with the intention of it being a one-off. They say that everyone has a book in them and that was supposed to be mine. After some lovely feedback, I decided to do a follow up called, 'Deadwater.' Maybe 'Broken Leaves' will be my last, who knows. All I can say is that writing has been a journey with many twists and turns, just like my books I suppose. In fact, just like life.

I was born in England and then lived in Wales and Northern Ireland before finally landing in Bonnie Scotland at the impressionable age of eight. I suppose you could call me multi-cultural but in a homely sort of way. My stories tend to be based in Scotland although for 'Deadwater' the location moved to the English/ Welsh border, a place I spent time in when I was young.

Reading has always been one of my great passions. I love books that build up a gothic atmosphere of foreboding, the first half of Dracula by Bram Stoker being a classic example. In my opinion, a good book should always have an unexpected finale. I will never forget reading 'Rebecca' by Daphne Du Maurier and the way the twist turned the whole story on its head.

I hope that by the time you have finished my book you will have enjoyed the journey into the dark corners of your imagination. As I mentioned before, we all have the potential to write a book. Maybe mine will inspire you to give it a go as well.

Dedicated to all those who liked to drink

but forgot to stop.

CONTENTS

What can you possibly give to the man who has everything? At first, it seems like a difficult question. But if you think about it, there can only be one answer. You let him choose the only gift he has never been given, self-destruction. That way you get to watch his life unravel, and the beauty of it is, he does it all by himself.

And the woman who has nothing? That one is easy.

You give her revenge.

CHAPTER ONE:
THE SPAGHETTI
INCIDENT

(Year Zero 1978)

Roni was the first to step out of the car. She was always more confident than me when we pulled this stunt, 'You have to act as though you do not have a care in the world, Matt. Show even a chink of self-doubt and they will know.' Her words of supposed encouragement would never help though. I would always follow into the shop with my stomach churning and my face a perfect picture of guilt.

I can still see the image of the premises, a typical small late 1970s general groceries store. No doubt a one-man operation, perfect for us. But as Roni's slim figure disappeared through the door and I did my usual count to twenty my eyes focused on the sign outside.

Birkby & Son General Groceries.

It was the son part that did it. Somehow it made me

feel that we would be stealing from real people rather than a shop. How I wish I had followed my instinct that day and waited until Roni realised, I had chickened out. 18,19,20 and with a sigh I opened the door of the battered old Mark II Cortina and tried to walk with some sort of confidence towards the entrance.

He was a small man with a protruding stomach and balding head. Probably in his mid-fifties but he could have been younger. When you are only 19, I suppose everyone over 30 looks ancient, well they did to me. Mr. Birkby, I assumed it was he, looked up from the counter and smiled at me. I went straight into my act, but I could feel the heat rising up my body and into my face. I could sense my cheeks growing red even as I spoke the agreed words. 'Julie, I need a box of matches, you get the crisps and I will have a wee smoke outside while I wait for you.' We had so little money that even the act of handing over cash to Birkby and his invisible son would only stretch to a few pence for a box of matches. My purchase was simply to hold the shopkeeper's attention. Behind the shelves, Roni would be filling her large coat with whatever we needed to keep us going until we got back to Glasgow. The problem with my accomplice was she tended to have a scattergun approach to shoplifting and would grab anything she could lay her hands on. Half of the stolen goods would end up being tossed out of the car window as we progressed North.

Maybe Liverpool grocery store owners are more cynical than motorway service station staff. As soon as I spoke, I could feel Birkby's eyes look right through me. That was the difference, stealing from a service station was like taking things from a faceless company. This was robbing from another human being. He looked around me and peered at the well-stocked shelves before shouting, 'What the fuck are you doing behind their young lady?' And that was when everything went completely pear-shaped. His reaction was far beyond what we expected, Christ it was only chocolate, crisps, wine, whatever we could get away with.

Birkby jumped the counter, maybe he was younger than I remember after all? Before I knew what was happening, he had grabbed Roni by the shoulders and ripped her coat open. Two bottles of wine fell to the ground and smashed into a sea of liquid and broken glass. They were followed by a waterfall of chocolate bars, biscuits, washing powder, rubber gloves, even a tin of spaghetti bounced into the pile. The three of us stood for a few seconds as if transfixed by the impressive amount of unpaid goods piled up on the floor. The odd thing is I remember thinking, *Roni, what the fuck are you stealing rubber gloves and a tin of spaghetti for? We don't even have a tin opener.*

It was Birkby who broke the spell first. His face was a picture of anger and rage. 'You robbing fucking Scottish bastards, Police, Police!!' He went to run back to the till, maybe he was going for the phone, I don't know. Don't ask me why I did it, I think it was just a nervous reaction. I was terrified, shit scared. *Bloody hell robbery, my dad would kill me.* As the shopkeeper turned, I stuck my foot out and in his blind fury, he went over my leg and crashed to the floor. It would have been ok if he had just fallen and allowed us to get the hell out of there but the bit that happened next was surreal. I kid you not, it was like watching a movie. *I was sitting in the comfy seats eating popcorn watching him fall in slow motion, down, down, down. Squelch and his body smashed into the broken glass followed by a loud bang as his head smacked the hard floor.*

Roni stood ashen-faced, rigid with total shock as we looked down at the motionless body of the shopkeeper. I knelt beside him, *Christ, he must be ok, it was only a fall, he will be fine.* We should have run then, got the hell away and maybe we could have pretended it never happened, forgotten all about it. But my natural instinct was to help him. I turned him over and felt sick with fear. At least three large pieces of the broken bottle protruded from his stomach as a deep red liquid gushed from his body and flowed into the grotesque mass of blood, wine, chocolate, and biscuits. And then we ran, ran out of that little shop of horrors and back into the car. Within seconds the old Cortina was flying up the road while inside its occupants wept with fear and shock.

I know you are sitting comfortably in your reading chair, shaking your head in disgust. *How could you leave a badly injured and innocent person to run away like that?* Look, I am not expecting sympathy but put yourself in my shoes. I was 19, dressed like a survivor from a nuclear war and standing over a man we might have killed. What would you have done? And don't forget, it was 1978 and we were from Glasgow. They would have locked us up and thrown away the key. Don't try and tell me you would not have run as well. I can even hear you panting as you try to keep up with me and Roni. Welcome to my nightmare.

(Glasgow Evening Times newspaper advert, 1978)

For Sale

**Mark II Cortina, 1968 model.
MOT until October 1978.**

A lovely little runner (If you can get it to start). Pale blue when new. (Now just pale) Three bald tyres but fourth still has legal tread. Spare tyre missing. (Itt got nicked when we went to Liverpool) Some rust on wings and rear tail light/bumper damaged. (Car rear-ended just outside Preston on the same trip as above) Extras include, Ashtray (Full), Speedometer (Broken), a tin of spaghetti (Unopened) and driver's seatbelt. (Passenger seatbelt missing). £25 ONO. Please note. Buyer collects. Car abandoned just outside Carlisle. (Fucker packed up on the way home).

CHAPTER TWO:
SUITS AND SAFETY
PINS

(2014)

*A*nd *now, the man we have all been waiting for. Please put your hands together and give your usual warm welcome to our UK Managing Director, Matt Cunningham.*

You would have thought that after more than 30 years with Blackbaron Technologies and 7 years at the top I would be at ease talking in front of 600 people. Not a chance. I might have looked calm, that was all the coaching and presentation courses that made me seem that way. Inside I was squirming or to put it bluntly, *I was shitting myself.* I would lay in bed the night before while Cara slept soundly beside me. My head would swim with words as I drifted into a half-sleep. Come the morning I would have completed the presentation twenty times over and feel like I had slept all night in a hedge.

I stood up from my seat at the front of the auditorium and walked over to shake hands with the site director Paul Fitzpatrick. As I turned to face the throng, I could feel a genuine warmth in the applause. How times change. In previous years when we had been downsizing things had been very different. Now the assembled sea of heads knew my time was almost over and maybe I was not such a bad guy after all. Most likely they would be thinking about my possible replacement. He would have to hit the ground running, make an early statement. Staff reduction would inevitably follow and then a pat on the back for the new boss plus a big bonus for reducing costs. I had done the same when I was given the top spot. You felt bad about it at the time, but a good round of golf would help you forget. I always felt it would be better for women to run companies, more compassion, and less muscle flexing. The presentation went fine, it always did despite my worries.

I stopped outside the driveway while the gates moved slowly apart. I should have felt good, the sun was shining, the hood was down on my white Merc. No sign of Cara, her car was gone. No doubt away to Pilates or coffee with the girls. Maybe she was even away seeing him, the guy I was not supposed to know about. Whitecraigs is an extremely affluent part of Glasgow and our home stood proudly amongst the bespoke country houses. Nothing here for you unless you have a spare few million hanging around. Look I know I am coming across as a big-headed shmuck but don't kid yourself. You would feel the same and yes, maybe I got lucky in my career. I still had to work my way up, I was not born with a silver spoon in my mouth you know. I can be tough, but I always tried to do what was fair. Anyway, no one likes the boss, it is a fact of life. Christ, I don't even like mine.

I edged the car slowly towards the large double garage at the end of the drive but still had to stop and wait for it to complete the opening ceremony. It annoyed me that the timer on the automatic door was not set correctly causing me to have to wait a few more seconds. *Was that what my life had become? Getting annoyed about the time it took a garage door to open.* Even though the entrance now beckoned me to drive forward, I sat in the car and did not move. It was as if the simple act of parking the Merc would signal the end of my life. A few more weeks and my early retirement would start, helped by a £1.5 million pay off. Golf every day followed by a few drinks, maybe enjoy the garden, have a game of snooker? If you had asked me how I felt about retiring a month ago I might have said I had mixed feelings. Now as I sat there, I had only one emotion and it was fear. The future had suddenly been grasped out of my hands. Matt Cunningham, the man who was always in control was suddenly lost at sea.

I finally managed to get the car into the garage and pressed my phone to close the door behind me. But still, I made no attempt to make the short journey through the connecting hallway into the house. It was the note I was thinking about. *Who the hell had written it and what did they want?* It had all started just two weeks ago, a personal letter sent to my work. I knew it was odd the minute I looked at the envelope. No one sends written letters these days unless they want something. I opened it with an increasing sense of unease. The single hand-written sentence sent a cold shudder down my spine. The words pointed at me like the accusing finger of a prosecution lawyer.

I know what you did all those years ago. It is time to stop running. V

Over the last two weeks, I had racked my brains trying to work out who it was. I checked every email, every text, the employee register for the whole of Blackbaron, our many friends and acquaintances, even our extended family including the ones we never spoke to. Nothing made any sense and the letter V gave no clues at all. I tried to convince myself that the reference to the past had nothing to do with the incident, but I knew was kidding myself.

I felt so powerless, something I was not used to. *Whoever it was, how much did they know and what did they want?* I prayed it was a friend or work colleague trying to wind me up. *Could the reference to the past just be a co-incidence?* I would play the game, maybe it was part of my leaving celebration? *Best go along with-it Matt, wait and see what happens. You have no choice.*

The next occurrence came a week later with a call to go to the reception area. I had put the letter to the back of my mind. Tried to pretend it meant nothing, convinced myself it had no connection with that day over 35 years ago. 'Hi Matt, there is someone to see you at the front desk. They say they have an appointment with you.' I headed across the vast expanse of corridors and offices of the Blackbaron Technologies plant towards the large glass fronted reception area. I had no recollection of agreeing to meet anyone that day but then my memory liked to taunt me for its own amusement. I was never sure if I forgot things because life had become so repetitive or it was down to age. I think I read a book about memory loss once, but I can't remember what it said.

'Hi Anne, you phoned to say someone was waiting to see me?'

'Oh no, it was not me Matt. It must have been Jane, she has just this second gone for lunch. I only took over a few minutes ago. She never mentioned anything about anyone waiting for you.' Both of us looked around at the seating area, it was empty. I suppose I should have followed up with the receptionist Jane at the time, but I just put it down to one of those things. Probably someone cold calling, maybe trying to sell the company a new training package or some other crap.

But it did not end there. A few days later I was sitting at my work desk sorting through the endless emails that arrived every few minutes. I would delete hundreds each day, just quickly scan through them for anything important. Most of it no longer mattered, very soon I would be gone and forgotten. Someone tapped me on the shoulder, and I turned around to see Barry Rae standing in front of me holding a pile of leaving cards.

'Ok boss, I hope you are not working too hard during

your last few weeks.' I liked Barry, he was a good manager, easy to work with, low maintenance. I think he hoped to get a shot at being my replacement, I already knew he had no chance.

'Hi Barry, what have you got there, you been promoted to head postman?'

We indulged in idle chat for a few minutes before he deposited at least 30 envelopes on my desk. I had gradually handed over most of my duties to other members of the management team until my replacement was announced. It felt strange to be wasting the hours away when the previous years had meant 70-hour week's just to keep the wolves from the door. I quickly glanced through the pile of cards without opening them. They would join the hundreds of others I had dumped in my briefcase. They meant nothing to me and somehow, I knew they meant little to the people who had sent them. As the cards cascaded between my fingers into the bag, I saw the letter. How could I miss it? A small white envelope, just like the first one. Tiny in comparison to the rest laying at the bottom of the case. I reached down and picked it out of the pile. That was the point that I finally realised that my past was back. I did not need to read the note inside, it was obvious what was coming.

I called into your work the other day. I know where you live as well, in fact, I know everything about you Cunningham, including what you did. Yes, even that. V

At least I now knew that the person who had called at reception was the same one sending me the letters. By the time I followed up with Jane the receptionist she had no recollection of who had been looking for me. No surprise I suppose, she dealt with hundreds of visitors each day. I considered asking security to see if they could identify who it was by looking back at the camera recordings, but I knew that would arouse suspicion and decided against it. *Surely It had to be some sort of blackmail?* Whoever it was, I would wait until they contacted me and pay whatever was required to make them disappear.

Mary, our house help was just finishing as I walked into the large kitchen. The place was spotless as always, Cara stressed about things being perfect. I suppose she had to, her world was dominated by keeping one up on her social circle. Our friends were the kind we had made once we had reached the top rather than met on the way. It was not as though we had ditched our old pals, it was just evolution. They had not moved on, but we had. 'Thanks Mary, the place looks amazing as always.'

'Cheers, Matt. If you could let Cara know I will be a wee bit early tomorrow that would be great.' I was just going through the motions listening to her while I scanned through the local newspaper that was delivered free each week.

'Oh ok, what's up? Have you got a wild night out planned?' Our home help had been with us for several years and would be the last person who would have a wild night scheduled. Mary was in her early fifties but unlike Cara, she obviously disliked health foods and Pilates classes. I liked her but in a nice old auntie kind of way. It's a human trait that we consider others as getting old rather than ourselves. We still have this mental picture in our heads of us when we were young. I was still that teenage punk, it was Mary who had let life wear her out, not me. The problem was, I was probably a few years older than her and when I looked in a mirror, I saw some old stranger staring back at me. Not even a hint of a Mohican and my thinning hair was white now rather than red.

'I wish I was going on a wild night out Matt. Unfortunately, I need to go to the home tomorrow afternoon to discuss the care arrangements for my mother.' As soon as she said the words, I felt guilty for making a joke. I should have remembered, Mary was always talking to Cara about the problems her aged mother was facing.

'Oh yes, of course, Mary, I was just kidding you. Let me know if we can help with anything?' The last bit was just a throwaway comment. Mary would be too proud to ask for anything she had not worked for. Don't get me wrong, I am not looking for a round of applause. I doubt I would give up my golf afternoon to visit her mum, but I would have given her money if she needed it. I am no angel though. I admit it, I have loads of the stuff, giving a little away now and then helped me feel a little saintly. Yes, Saint Matt of Whitecraigs, he gave 1% of his millions to middle-aged ladies with sick mothers.

'Did you get the mail? The box at the gate was nearly full when I went out to collect it. Right, that's me, Matt, I will see you tomorrow.' Mary put on her coat and walked off towards the back door. Her little car would be sitting beside my Merc, The Range Rover and our daughter Simone's Sporty BMW. Surrounded by polished affluence while it waited for its next MOT.

I was already logging onto my laptop even before Mary had started the engine of her car. I scanned through the endless emails, most of them telling me how much I would be missed. *It has been an honour and a pleasure to be in your team Matt, happy retirement when it comes and keep in touch.* It was all false though, well maybe a few really meant it. The rest would be trying to flatter me, hoping I would recommend them to the new boss. I just sat there, working methodically down the screen, delete, delete, delete. I knew I would be gone and forgotten in a matter of weeks, that was how life was in every workplace. In fact, that was how life was, full stop. Once you leave, you leave and that includes planet earth. Unless you are as well off as me and you get your own little plot with a memorial. Maybe then you are remembered for a little while longer, at least until the local yobs come to kick the gravestones over.

I made a cup of tea, called my long-time friend Eric, fed the cat and waited. The kitchen clock ticked, and the silence gradually consumed me. And then the words came back into my head, the words Mary had uttered as she left.

Did you get the mail? the box was nearly full when I went to collect it.

I walked through the house to the hallway. Towards the pile, more cards, junk mail and there it was. Another little letter addressed to me. This was getting serious, not only did V know where I worked, they had my home address as well. I ignored everything else and returned to the kitchen before I slowly started to tear the envelope open. *Please God, let this be the punchline to the joke or at least a demand for cash.* Something I could fix, something I could control, something I could defeat with money.

'Hi Matt, what are you doing home so early? Put the kettle on, I am dying for a cuppa.' I nearly fell off the fucking kitchen stool.

'For fuck sake Cara, you scared the shit out of me. What the fuck are you doing sneaking in like a bloody ghost? I was concentrating on my laptop, you nearly gave me a fucking heart attack.' Can I just point out that I do not normally swear at my wife. I was in a stressful situation and she did frighten the crap out of me. Ok, ok, I know it was unintentional, don't make me feel any worse than I already do.

'Jeez Matt, you are such a bloody drama queen. I bet you don't speak to your work colleagues like that. Make me a coffee darling while I go up and get a shower.' She disappeared through one of the doors, a vision of sophistication and lycra. I was already ignoring her words though, my eyes focusing on the little note.

Cunningham. The time has come to stop running. You

are a murderer and now you must pay. V

The past had returned, my nightmare was just beginning. How ironic that my start would come back to haunt me when I was so close to my end.

Talking about the past....

(1978)

The van was in front of us with Calum, Tobi, and the band's equipment. I followed behind in the Cortina with Roni. The car was a nightmare, but we had no choice other than to take it as Tobi's van was jammed solid with our equipment. Well, most of the space was taken up with his drum kit to be fair but it was his van after all. Roni's cousin Craig let us take his car, I think he was glad to see the back of it. It had neither an MOT nor insurance, but that did not bother us. I only had a provisional license anyway and Roni did not drive. I was amazed we did not get pulled over by the cops as the Cortina looked like a travelling scrap yard. In a strange way, the horrible wet weather was a bonus for us I reckon. The pouring rain and mist helped to hide the car or maybe the police did not like to get wet. They probably just stayed beside the heater at the police station and played cards for the weekend. It was the seventies after all. I don't think job accountability started until at least 1984. Once Maggie Thatcher had sunk the boot into the miners then everyone had to do real work.

Don't laugh but the name of the band was Social Decline. It was Tobi's band really, he was the only one who could play. He was older than us, maybe about 25 and had been in various bands before. I think he saw the punk thing as a chance to jump on the bandwagon and make some money. Calum played the bass, well he hit the strings in some sort of random order and pretended he knew what he was doing. I was on guitar, I could play about 3 or 4 chords and that was it. Roni was our singer, she looked great but sounded like a dying cat. Liverpool was only our second gig, the first had been in Kilmarnock near Glasgow. Roni lived with her mum in the town, so she managed to sweet talk the bar manager into giving us the chance to play in the local pub. About ten males turned up and ogled Roni all night while wishing the three guys backing her would stop making a racket.

The trip to Liverpool was a big deal for Tobi as Social Decline had been given the support slot to a popular local punk band. I think he only got the gig because of previous contacts. In the weeks up to the journey, Tobi had been a pain in the arse trying to get us to practise. The truth was that me, Calum and Roni just wanted to laugh and get drunk as most 19-year-olds do. Well, Roni was only 16 but she carried a self-confident aura that made her seem older. God, it still makes me go red when I think back to that night in Liverpool. We even gave ourselves punk names to spruce our image up. I was known as Mattress. It was a play on my name and the fact that I liked to sleep until midday. Roni was Roni Wreckage because she was an absolute fruit loop. She was small and lightly built but she could handle herself better than a six-foot boxer. Calum was Spider, I have no idea why. We tried to talk Tobi into having a punk name, but he was too aloof and liked to pretend he was an adult. 'Hey Tobi, you need a new moniker before we go to Liverpool, you can't be a punk with a name like Tobi.'

'There is fuck all wrong with being called Tobi. I reckon that is the last thing a paying audience is going to be bothered about. If you fuckers would concentrate on playing your instruments and trying to sing it might fucking help.' He was such an easy guy to wind up, so I continued pushing him.

'We are supposed to be punks, they are not meant to be able to play properly.'

'For fuck sake Matt, there is not playing properly and not being able to play at all! It is a big fucking difference. How about you learn another fucking chord and stop worrying about what my fucking name should be.' Roni jumped in to ramp things up a bit.

'How about Tobi the Cock or Tobi the Virgin?' Calum was next in.

'How about Tobi or not Tobi, that is the question?'

Our band leader shrugged his shoulders and told us to fuck off. Whether he liked it or not though, from that day on he was The Virgin to the rest of the band.

I was in love with Roni in those days, how could I not be? She was fucking crazy and just great fun to be with. For some reason, she insisted we pull off the motorway into some godforsaken village called Sammington in the Scottish Borders. She had seen a sign pointing to Bruce's cave. It was supposed to be the famous hiding place of King Robert the Bruce of Scotland when he was on the run from the English in 1306.

'Roni, for fuck sake, there are probably hundreds of places that claim to be the cave he hid in. Anyway, The

Virgin will have a fit if we do not keep following his van.'

'Fuck the Virgin, I want to see the cave. Follow that sign.' When Roni wanted to do something you just had to go with it. She would do things on a whim and her enthusiasm would be impossible to ignore.

We stood on the wet wooden platform that skirted high above the swollen stream at the mouth of the cave. She held onto the fragile looking fence that separated us from the 100-foot drop into the angry water. Roni's eyes sparkled with joy as she peered down into the depths. 'Roni, you are giving me the fear, come back a bit, it's slippy you fucking nutcase.'

'You are such a moan, Matt, look at the water. How beautiful it is, crashing and bouncing against the rocks. Free to do whatever it wants. Just think, we could take one step and leap together into another world.' She turned around and stared at me, her face innocent and happy. Then she threw herself onto me causing the two of us to fall backwards into the cave. Both of us laughing as we collapsed into each other's arms. A frozen moment in time that could never be captured again.

We pulled into a garage somewhere near the Lake District

in the pouring rain. Roni jumped out and ran to the van to try and get some money from The Virgin for petrol. The problem was we had to keep the car running all the time as the battery was flat and it would not start again unless we pushed it. Tobi would ration the money out, mainly for petrol to make sure we made it to the gig. Within minutes a soaking and bedraggled Roni jumped back in the car. 'Miserable bastard would only give me a fiver for petrol. I think he is scared we will run off to a pub if he gives us anymore. He probably is a virgin, the tight arsed git.'

'Christ Roni, I am starving. Let's spend a quid on food and the rest on petrol, he is not going to know the difference.'

'You kidding? Don't worry about food Matt, no point in spending money on that. Pull up at that wee shop over there.'

And that was the first time we did the shoplifting stunt. Roni was an absolute expert at it. Within minutes I was walking out of the little store having spent 5 pence on matches. Meanwhile, Roni had put on an extra two stone as she waddled out with a week's shopping supply under her coat. We did this at least four times before arriving in Liverpool that night and even had enough to pass onto the rest of the band in exchange for a joint. Now I wish that we had got caught earlier and maybe life would have been different. Maybe Birkby would still be alive or at least have had the chance to grow into old age.

I think the gig was in a pub called The Sportsman. The minute we walked in our faces dropped. It looked so big and professional, I just knew we were going to be out of our depth. Even Tobi looked scared although I don't think it was the venue that frightened him, it was the rest of the band he would have to play with. We had no money to stay anywhere so it left us five hours to kill before we went on stage. The plan was to have a few drinks after the show and then sleep in the van outside the place. The pub manager offered to let us leave our gear in the premises overnight.

We set our equipment up and made a pathetic attempt to sound check but even after all that we still had hours left with nothing to do. 'Hey Tobi, how about giving us a few quid for some drinks? It is pissing down outside, we can't sit here all afternoon doing nothing.' I asked the question knowing full well that the tight arsed bastard would not give us a penny.

'Aye right. You three are fucking useless enough without being drunk as well. NO drinking before the gig. I am heading into Liverpool city centre to see a mate. Maybe

I will get an offer to go back to a real fucking group rather than you school kids. Now be good children and behave yourselves.' With that caustic insult, The Virgin disappeared out of the pub door to go and do whatever he was going to do. I am sure if he had known just how bad our gig would go, he would not have bothered coming back.

'What the fuck are we going to do now?' Roni looked bored. That was never a good sign, it could only mean trouble.

'If we had enough money to just go home, I would jump at it. Tobi is a fucking dick, he could have left us a few quid at least.'

But divine intervention was walking towards us in the shape of the pub manager.

'Guys, I will pay you cash up front now. Things will get very busy in here later and I do not want to be fucking around looking for you lot. Just make sure you put on a good show but not too good in case you piss the main act off. Where is Tobi?

I jumped in quickly just in case the miracle disappeared.

'He has just nipped out for a while. He said you should deal with me if it is anything to do with the band being paid up front.' The manager looked at me with what could only be suspicion.

'Mmmm, are you sure? I thought Tobi was in charge?'

'Yes, he is, but he is my older brother, so he lets me look after things when he needs help,' I lied.

'Your older brother? You look nothing fucking like him. For a start off he is three feet taller than you.' Just my luck that the bar manager would turn out to be a comedian as well.

'He is my half-brother, same mother, different fathers. His old man was a giraffe and mine was a pigmy.' I think the manager liked me as he smiled but he still held onto the money as though he was not convinced.

'You can give it to me Sir, if you want. I am Tobi's older sister, we are really close.' Roni spoke the words while mimicking the voice of a little girl lost. I thought she had blown it, but the manager was now laughing heartily.

'You are a cocky little bunch of fuckers, I will give you that.' I think he was taken with Roni, it was hard not to be.

'So, you are his older sister, are you?' He was still laughing as he handed her the £30 gig money.

'Listen little lady. Make sure you get that money to Tobi. All of it and don't fucking mess me about.'

The three of us stared at the massive amount of cash

and then looked at each other. We knew what had to be done. There is a saying, *don't shit on your own doorstep*, so we walked for ten minutes in the rain to the next pub. I tried to take over as the bandleader and be the adult in the absence of our boss The Virgin.

'Ok guys, Just a couple of beers. We need to be a tight unit on stage tonight. This could be the big one.' Roni looked at me and burst out laughing.

'Fuck off Matt. Don't give me that crap. Who the fuck do you think you are, Eric Clapton?' She grabbed the thirty pounds out of my hands and burst through the door of the pub. A girl on a mission, followed by two boys needing little persuasion.

Like most big drinking sessions, I cannot really remember what happened. I do recall one thing though. I and Calum had a pool competition and the final score sticks in my memory. You see even then I was a competitive bastard. I had to win at pool the same way I needed to have the perfect golf handicap 36 years later. You can visualise how much we had to drink by the fact that I won 13-4. That is 17 games of fucking pool! I think at one-point Roni knocked a full glass of beer all over the pool table. We mopped it up while our singer zigzagged her way to the bar to order a last round. She crashed into another table sending more drinks flying. The barman had been concentrating on serving another customer when he heard the commotion. 'Right you lot, out now. Fucking move it and don't come back.' Roni managed to stand up although she had difficulty balancing on the same spot.

'Hold onto your fucking horse Mister Bartender. We were just leaving anyway, we have a gig to do in ten minutes. We are a famous fucking rock band from Scotland, you should be honoured to have us in your establishment.' I think that is what she said or tried to say. Even though I was in a bad way, it dawned on me that Roni was completely pissed. I grabbed hold of her and the three of us bounced out of the pub.

'Any chance I can get your autograph, Lulu.' The shouted comment from the barman was lost on us as we merged back out into the wet street.

We staggered back to The Sportsman with less than a fiver left of our gig money. Tobi went absolutely fucking mental. He was literally frothing at the mouth at the condition we were in as well as having drunk away most of the money. He had no choice though; the place had filled up and they wanted a band to warm them up. So, pissed or not we got on the stage to give them a show. Maybe not the sort of show they expected if truth be told.

Tobi sat at his drums and leaned into his mic. 'We are Social Decline and we do not give a fuck!' That was our planned punk introduction and then he would smash into the drums followed by me and Calum on our guitars. The first few seconds started ok, but it was when Roni went to grab the mic and start caterwauling that things went badly wrong. She was so drunk her hands missed the stand and she staggered forwards before toppling over and off the stage. The guitars stopped as we stared at our spread-eagled singer, only Tobi kept the beat going with his drums but even they died after another few seconds. To be fair to Roni she did manage to jump up, maybe too quickly though as she staggered backwards this time and once more lost her footing. No wonder we christened her Roni Wreckage, she took out most of Tobi's drums as she came down. It was fascinating to watch someone so small cause so much damage. I looked at the sizeable audience wondering what they thought of the show, but they were no longer looking at Roni. I turned just in time to see Calum throw up like an endless waterfall all over the stage.

The manager threw us and our gear out in the street.

The last I saw of Tobi was him loading his drum kit in the van and driving off. Calum staggered away, we did not see our bass guitarist again until we got back to Glasgow. I seem to remember he told me he slept in a park and then hitch-hiked home. I and Roni spent the night packed like sardines in the car with the guitars and other equipment. The plan was to sell it when we got back home, Social Decline was over before it had started.

We woke the next day hung over and freezing cold. I reckon we were still very drunk. Year Zero had arrived. Maybe our first stop on the way home at Birkby & Son General Grocer would have gone ok if we had been sober. But as I already explained, if you thought the gig was bad then what happened in the little store was far worse.

I think me, and Roni only lasted together for three months after the Liverpool debacle. I was in love with her but although we never mentioned the incident it was still there. You could feel, see, smell Birkby everywhere we went. In the end, we had to separate to release the tension and escape into a new life. I missed her, you never forget your first love I suppose. The last time I saw her would be three years later. By then I had almost finished my degree at university and was starting to make my way in life. It was in a crowded bar in Glasgow, I was with my new college friends. She looked amazing. Despite being the smallest amongst the group of women she was with, she still stood out. For a fleeting few seconds, we caught each other's eyes through the throng of evening drinkers. She waved and smiled at me. I nodded quickly and turned away. I could tell she was drunk.

Even though I would not admit it, I slowly cut out everyone from my punk days. The fear of the tap on the shoulder receded with every old friend I cast adrift as the months and years went by. Some long-forgotten conversation in a pub mentioned that Roni had ended up with a drinking problem and no one knew what had happened to her. She slid from my memory as each year passed. I did occasionally see Calum, a nice guy but even he faded away. God knows what happened to Tobi, maybe he really did change his name to The Virgin and become famous?

(2014)

I stared at the little piece of paper with the words written on it. Who the hell was V? Not a single friend or acquaintance remained from year zero, no possible link with the past that had not been severed. Even in my memory, it had been locked away into a vault, never to be re-visited. And yet, that one sentence written in black ink had the power to destroy every one of my defences. A few words and I was back outside that shop, running for my life with Roni following close behind. I had always kidded myself that Birkby did not die. He had been knocked unconscious from the fall. A few cuts having landed on the broken glass, blood always makes things look worse.

I walked back and forwards across the kitchen floor, every nerve in my body pulsing with shock. Surrounded by normality, pristine white kitchen units, flowers, the clock ticking away the seconds of my life. Cara came back from her shower. A vision of normality with her wet hair flowing down the side of her dressing gown. 'You made the coffee yet grumpy pants? I had better get used to you being under my feet I suppose. Only another few weeks and you can join me and the girls at the exercise class.' She kissed me on the cheek, a quick act of forced closeness. Within seconds she was heading away again, onto her next phone call or coffee meeting. I had been instantly dismissed as she charged on with her busy life.

The words buzzed around in my head. My mind tried to re-arrange them, attempt to make them mean something else. Transform them into something that would fit and make sense. Blend in with the tea towels, the ornament's, the dripping tap. But no, the words had been carved in rock now. They could never be erased. I could maybe buy some more time, pay my way to a further reprieve but the statue had been sculpted. Its finger pointing firmly in my direction for all to see.

Cunningham. The time has come to stop running. You are a murderer and now you must pay. V

(Liverpool Music Scene Magazine review, 1978)

Have I just witnessed the worst or the funniest band I have ever seen play, Liverpool? Local punk stars The Guilty Dogs where the main attraction for the sizeable crowd who turned out at The Sportsmen last Tuesday. More about their excellent set later but first on was Glasgow's newest punks Social Decline.

I have no idea who the rest of this catastrophic act is, but the drummer is one Tobi Kingston who at one time played with semi-famous hippy rock band Dragonesque. Do you want to bet that Mr. Kingston has hit hard times and decided to throw a young punk band together in the hope he can grab a bit of the current scene? The reality is, he is a boring old hippy fart and the kids he had along with him are about as punk as Fred Astaire.

The comedy part? That came when Social Decline managed three chords into their first song before the cute but clearly drunk female singer fell off the stage and then recovered only to crash backwards into the drum kit. How can someone so small cause so much carnage? I am sure the bass player was throwing up as well when the lights went down. Great effort Tobi, now piss off back to Razor city with your pathetic plastic punk band and try to remember next time. This is Liverpool, birthplace of The Beatles and we still have some self-respect in our music scene.

CHAPTER THREE:
POUR YOURSELF
ANOTHER, RONI

(2014)

It was 3 o'clock in the morning and my head was buzzing. No matter how hard I tried or how many different sleeping positions I adopted, I remained wide awake. Cara breathed quietly alongside, a picture of normality in a world that had crashed and burned around me. I looked at her and felt guilty. Who the hell was V and how much detail did they have? If they really did know what had happened in my past, then why not simply blackmail me? Tell me what they wanted and be done with it. Christ, I would pay whatever was needed, why all the mystery? The obvious answer was that my blackmailer wanted me to suffer, wanted to make me feel like a fool before either destroying me or bleeding me dry.

How I wished I could go back to normality, back to

my position as the supplier of the equilibrium. Cara and Simone deserved it, they had played their part in getting us to the final chapter. If it had just been me, I could have faced the horror, accepted my fate. But this was everything, the family, our status, our history, even our epitaph. And, our shame. The fall out would impact all three of us equally even though the girls had not even entered my life before that day. Christ, I would even accept Cara having her affair if I could go back to playing golf and drifting into old-age but it was too late now. And, the reality was, I was being a coward the way I had always been from the day we had run from Birkby's shop. I knew that if my past came out, I would be going to jail. Christ, at my age! They would eat me alive.

At last, I started to drift into sleep, a confused contortion of images and words floating and fading. Fuck, I was wide awake again! It had hit me like an express train. *What an idiot, of course, it is so fucking obvious.* All evening and well into that long night my head had rattled about between shock and trying to be logical. I had played over and over reasons, random thoughts. *Who could it be? Had Birkby survived and tracked me down? Had he died and now at long last his son had traced me? Who was it, who would know?* And the answer had been standing there in front of me all the time. A statue of a forgotten past staring at me, pointing the finger of guilt. It was her, wasn't it? The only other person who knew what happened that day.

She was back, Roni was coming home after more than 35 years of being a distant shadow. No doubt looking for a piece of my success, ready to stake her claim. That must be it, *she is going to blackmail me.* And for the first time since I had read the note, I could hear my breathing again. I could see the darkness recede and daylight peer once more into my brain. *If the dirty old drunk needs money, then she can have whatever she wants. Take it, I have tons of the stuff. Fuck you, Roni. Take your blood money but just let me get back to normality. Christ, I will even enjoy afternoon gin and old age so long as you disappear again and take Birkby with you.* And, the real relief was that it was now obvious that she could never really hand me in. She was as guilty as me, a quick pay off to the bitch and I could sink back into my comfort and retirement.

The white Merc was flying down the M77 to Kilmarnock. Time was against me, I had to find her before she went too far and arrived on my doorstep. I had paid to get my mail re-directed but she could just as easily send an email to Blackbaron Technologies. That was obviously how she had tracked me down. It would have been easy, my face was splashed all over the internet, the local papers, even the occasional slot on the television business news. I was a minor celebrity in the corporate world by simply being head of a massive business. She would have watched me, her mouth drooling with vodka while she slouched in her hovel. Smiling as she realised that the next bottle would come free, the next million bottles would come free. Her old partner in crime was obviously so stinking rich and successful that he was going to be her golden ticket. I had not seen Roni for years but now I hated her, hated every inch of her drink-sodden soul. How she must have laughed as she blagged her way into the reception at Blackbaron and then quickly disappeared again. I could just see her slugging drinks while she chuckled and typed away. Slowly building up to the punchline.

Cunningham. The time has come to stop running. You are a murderer and now you must pay. V

I was surprised at how easy it was to tell the chiefs at Blackbaron that I was taking my second last week with the company as leave. They made a pretence at being disappointed, but I could sense already that I was yesterday's man. The new UK head of operations was going to be announced tomorrow and everyone was moving into first gear to make sure they impressed him. No doubt he would want to spend some time talking to me, pretend he was interested in my view of things. I was beginning to feel like one of those pensioners in a home. People talking to me as though I was a child or a dog about to be put down. Maybe Roni had come to my rescue. Given me an excuse to get away from being treated like a kid for another week. 'We have a few dinner engagements planned for you Matt, oh and I think the Cardiff site wants to do a surprise presentation.'

'Well, I will still have one more week when I come back, Trevor. Maybe it will help the new guy find his feet without me getting in the way. I can then give him some quality time on my return.' I sensed that Trevor could feel something was wrong. I suppose it was so unlike dependable Matt not to follow every plan to the letter of the law.

'Alright, Matt. But you know you are such a big part of Blackbaron, I hope you don't feel the need to get out of the way. There are so many people who wish to see you before you finish.'

I came up with a story about my daughter Simone moving into a new flat and having problems. 'Well, you guys will just have to make it a great last week for me when I get back.'

It was agreed that on my return I would spend my final day's visiting each site to shake hands and say goodbye. A dinner for 120 invited UK managers and senior heads was planned as my finale. No doubt I would be presented with some glass ornament with my name inscribed on it. Something else to stick in the attic with the rest of the mementoes from my working life. You are probably thinking to your yourself, *God, what an ungrateful bastard.* You are right, but what the hell else could I do? I had some half-crazy drunken old hag on my case, and she was about to tell the world that I was a murderer. I could have accepted being blackmailed by anyone else, but memory told me that Roni Paterson was crazy when she was sixteen. Just imagine what she must be like now. An unstable old alcoholic who probably hated me for being a success.

It had been harder to convince Cara and Simone that I was disappearing for a week. 'I don't understand Matt, why? You cannot just go off on your own, what is up with you?' I should have just told them I was going to The US on a business trip, they would have accepted that as normal. But going away by myself for no reason!

'Look, Cara, there is nothing sinister in it, I just want

a week to adjust. A week of solitude. Surely after years of pressure, it is reasonable to take some time out, clear my head and get ready to embrace retirement?'

'Oh, for heaven's sake Matt. Will you ever grow up? Simone is already worried about you, she is going to wonder what the hell is wrong. Normal men take their family on a holiday when they retire. You decide to go off on some crazy hill walking adventure by yourself.' As usual, it ended in an argument and me sulking in my study.

Cara and Simone finally agreed with my plan, but I could tell they too knew something was not right. I had been away solo before. I had even taken a week to walk the West Highland way on my own a few years back. But they knew this was different, out of character, not normal. Call it a woman's intuition. To be fair my daughter Simone was genuinely concerned, I think Cara was already planning her clandestine visits to see him even before I walked out of the door that morning.

I had decided to base myself in Kilmarnock for the week, a peripheral town about twenty miles from Glasgow. I suppose it was a long shot, but I knew that was the place Roni had been brought up. Ok, the name Paterson was fairly common but maybe her parents or relatives still stayed in the vicinity. Look, I will be honest with you. The hotel in Kilmarnock was just to give me a base, somewhere not too far away. Did you really think I was going to search for her on my own? Don't be ridiculous, I already told you. I have money, loads of the fucking stuff. And for once, I really needed it.

Charles Cameron Ilderton was his name. I liked that, it sounded like the kind of name a private detective would have. He even looked like a larger more rotund version of that old American TV Cop, Columbo. He wore an old suit, creased and stained with years of slouching, smoking and talking too much. He came highly recommended by my best friend Eric. He had used him in his divorce case some years back. Again, I made up a story, even to my closest mate. I told Eric I needed a sleuth to track Cara as I was convinced, she was having an affair. That was a big lie as I knew damn fucking well, she was having an affair. In fact, I was sure that she knew that I knew she was seeing someone else. We had reached that point where we accepted it but pretended it was not happening.

Anyway, back to Charles Cameron Ilderton. At first, he told me he could not take on the case for at least a few weeks as he was busy.

'Yes, I understand Mr. Cunningham, you need to find this Roni Paterson urgently. But, trust me on this one. Finding a person after thirty-five years is not easy. I will need at least a week to work on the case and as I have already said. I cannot start until next month at the earliest. I am really sorry.'

'Look, Charlie, money is no object. I will pay you whatever it takes.'

'Yes Mr. Cunningham, but money is not the issue. If I had all the money in the world would it make me a better man? Can money buy contentment, Mr. Cunningham? Can it move you any higher up the pecking order when you come to meet the good Lord at the pearly gates? That is the question I will ask of you, Mr. Cunningham. That is the question.' The only thing I was asking myself was, *why the hell did Eric recommend this guy? He is fucking crazy.*

'I will take on your case but not for a few weeks. I am afraid it is a matter of take it or leave it. I have other customers and I simply cannot let them down. There is old Maggie Rodriguez, I am in the middle of a very sad job. She is sure that her old boy Ferdinand is having an affair with a twenty-year-old. Hard to believe, I know, as Ferdinand is in his eighties.' I jumped in and interrupted him before he could go on. It was becoming obvious that Charlie liked to talk. The kind of person who spoke a lot but said fuck all.

'Can I ask you a question, Charlie? How much would it cost me?'

'Well, if you agree to let me work for you and you accept that I will start next month. That is the start of next month rather than mid-month or at the end of the month. My fee would be £75 per hour. It will probably take me at least 2 or 3 days to track her using the internet and public records. Let us say approximately £1800 plus a finding fee of £500.' He pondered for a few seconds. This would prove to be unusual for Charles Cameron Ilderton as he rarely took a breath between sentences.

'Mr. Cunningham, as you are a friend of Eric's I will do it for a flat £2000. That is exactly £2000, not a penny more, bang on £2000 exactly. No find, no fee but starting in a few weeks because I am working on the Rodriguez case. Did I tell you about this one…'? My patience was wearing thin, so I cut his endless rambling off mid-sentence.

'Charlie, can I ask you to stop talking just for a minute, if you would be so kind? Let me put this straight to you. You start now, you find where she lives within two days. I will pay 5k up front and another 5k when you give me her address.'

'I should have her located within 36 hours Mr. Cunningham, leave it with me.'

And they say that money talks! Of course, it fucking does. I was meeting Charles Cameron Ilderton tonight at my hotel. He had found the dark-hearted blackmailing bitch within a day. I was hoping she was still local, and I could challenge her tomorrow. Give the old cow what she wanted, pay her off. Just like Charlie boy.

I lay on the bed in the hotel room reflecting on the 36 years that had passed since year zero. Maybe I was a success but, I knew I was just a cheap fraud. How dare I stand in front of hundreds of honest people and pontificate about being part of a team and working together. The man who had run and left his victim to die so he could save his own skin. *Please put your hands together for our well known and popular UK leader, Mr. Matt Cunningham.* They should have been booing me, not applauding. I jumped up as my phone kicked into life. Everyone except Charles Cameron Ilderton had been muted on my mobile. Nothing else in the world mattered other than to find that scheming old hag Roni before she could do any more damage.

'I am down at the reception Mr. Cunningham. I will

wait for you in the bar.' I tried to act calm as I waited for the lift to collect me on the third floor. By the time I arrived downstairs I was frothing at the mouth. I almost started shouting at him from across the room.

'Have you found her Charlie? Tell me you have found her? And for fuck sake stop calling me Mr. Cunningham. The name is Matt. I will give you another fiver if I must pay you more to use my real name. Mr. Cunningham makes me sound like a fucking school teacher.' I felt bad being so sharp with him. I am not normally so rude but Christ, give me a break, I was in a corner. I felt like someone was standing beside me with a stopwatch. When time ran out and they clicked it, a drunken Roni would be screaming in the middle of the street. *It's him, yes, it's him, he is a fucking murderer.*

'Yes Mr. Cunn, I mean Matt. I have some very good news for you.'

He was sitting at a secluded table in the corner of the hotel bar. Why do most hotel receptions and bar's always look so nondescript? It is if they have paid some designer to use as little imagination as possible to make the place look almost like a cheap television setting.

I know he was an odd character, but I was starting to warm to Charles Cameron Ilderton. Not only did his name sound like a private detective but he smoked like a chimney. He wore a suit but always looked dishevelled and stank of tobacco. His hair looked long and unkempt, far too long for a guy who must be at least sixty. He did talk too much but even that was kind of endearing. He was halfway through a pint of lager even though he must have driven up to meet me. I ordered a coffee and tried to calm down before sitting opposite the intrepid private investigator.

'Ok Charlie, what have you got?' He leaned forward like a true professional before speaking.

'Roni Paterson. Yes, she is still alive, in her early fifties now by all accounts.'

I wanted to say, *fuck me Charlie boy, I could have told you that for a lot less than the fortune I am paying you.* But I kept quiet and listened with respect to P.I. Ilderton.

'She left Kilmarnock in the early nineties I believe, never married but it was rumoured she had a drinking problem. I know she had a run in with the police a few times. The odd thing is she disappeared off the radar for nearly twenty years before re-appearing back in Scotland around 2009.'

'Look, Charlie, I really don't mean to be rude, but I am not interested in her life story. I just want to know where she is living now. Is it close?' But Charlie boy was on a roll and intended to build up to the punchline.

'Where the hell she was between leaving the country and coming back I have no idea. My European contact is working on it for me though. I will find out soon enough. I might just need a little more time to be able to flesh out my research Mr. Cunningham, I mean Matt.' By now my patience was wearing thin.

'Charlie, watch my fucking lips. Where the fuck is, she living now? I do not give a damn what she has been doing in the last twenty years or what the fuck your European contact finds out. Where is she...NOW? Is it close to Kilmarnock?'

'Yes Matt, well close is a very relative term. I mean Kilmarnock is close to Glasgow if you are driving but try telling me it is close if you are on foot. Let us just say she is not in Australia.' I gave him my best impatient glare. Christ did this guy ever get to the point.

'Yes, Yes, so where the fuck is, she living?' He took a deep breath, I felt like offering him an Oscar, he was hamming it up so much.

'Bendrennon cottage Matt, Bendrennon cottage.' He sat back and smiled, a look of triumph across his face as he took a long drink of his lager.'

'Ben fucking where? Is it close to Glasgow or

Kilmarnock? Charlie, I need more detail, where is it.' He leaned forward again and waited a few seconds before delivering his next piece of information. Maybe he felt guilty at taking 10 grand off me and had the need to make out as though he had worked hard for it. I would have paid him 50 grand if he had asked, so long as he found her.

'BENDRENNON.' He emphasised each letter as he spoke the words.

'Bendrennon. Yes, Yes, where is it, where is it?' By now I was ready to jump out of my seat and strangle the words out of him.

'Bendrennon, Matt, is North of Kinlochbervie at the North West tip of Scotland. I believe it is part of the very edge of the county of Sutherland.'

My brain was working in overdrive as I sat there. Leave at 4 in the morning and I could be confronting her by late afternoon. But I already knew I would be going straight away. No time to wait, drive overnight, get her before she had even woken up in the morning. Charlie boy had more, I knew he felt he had ripped me off and was throwing in some extras.

'She moved to a cottage on her own when she came back some years ago. I found out that she is known to the locals but is very reclusive. A hippy type, you get a lot of them up in the wilderness. Anyway, I will get the missing information on her life story for you whether you want it or not. All part of the service Matt. Is there anything else I can do for you?'

I know you are going to think I am fucking crazy and I don't even know why I did it, but I did. I leaned forward to look old Charlie boy right in the eyes as though I was some sort of Russian Spy.

'Yes, there is Charlie, indeed there is. Can you get hold of a small gun for me, a pistol, something I can hide easily in my coat? Plus, I want to keep you on a retainer. You work for me for the next two weeks, solely for me. I might not need you but then again I might, so you ignore all calls except for my number.' Charles Cameron Ilderton squinted his eyes at me and frowned. I had expected him to be shocked at my request, but he was looking at me as an equal. It was almost as if he was enjoying his job for the first time in years. Maybe he had only ever worked on endless potential divorce cases. Sitting in a steamed-up car in the rain while waiting to take a picture of his victim in an embrace with a lover. I am 100% certain none of his previous clients had asked him to get a gun.

'I will pay you the 10k we agreed for finding Miss Paterson. I will also pay you a further 25k at the end of the two weeks whether I use your services or not. Plus, 25k now for the gun. Oh, and bullets, just a few will be fine.' Charlie boy leaned even closer to me, so close I could smell his tobacco-stained breath. He took his usual few seconds before formulating his reply. But for a change, no words came. He simply held out his hand to shake mine and that was it. He was now my hired hand. It felt good, Butch Cassidy and The Sundance Kid. Christ, I was even getting a fucking gun!

Cara emptied the boiling water into the cup. She rarely stopped to think about things, life was too busy. A constant buzz of exercise classes, lunches with her many friends and pandering to her twenty-year-old daughter. It was as if she was scared to slow down and face the reality that her marriage and life as she knew it was sliding towards oblivion. As each year passed, she and Matt shared fewer words and virtually no physical contact. It was as if they were afraid to talk about anything serious in case it forced them to face the inevitable. But you cannot live with someone for 35 years and not care about them. Maybe it was guilt, but Cara still worried about Matt.

Her daughter Simone walked into the kitchen. She had recently turned 20, a young woman but in many ways still a child. Like most, at that age, she spoke and acted like an adult but would give her youthful innocence away with the occasional overreaction or comment.

'Mum, I don't understand. Why is dad away on his own? I mean where is he away too? Mum, I am worried about him.'

'Simone, I am not sure, to be honest.' For once Cara sounded tired and jaded. 'I think your dad is going through a bit of a late-life crisis. I know he has been acting odd lately, but he will get over it. Give him time to settle into not working and he will be fine.'

As all mothers did, she tried her best to ease her child's concerns even if she herself was not convinced. Cara wondered if Matt was having an affair, but the evidence did not stack up. He was too easy to get hold of, always with people on business or at golf. *It was not that, it was something else.* She had always known Matt was immature despite his high-flying job, *but then surely most men remain locked in their teenage years? Was it just a fear of growing old? Maybe he was having an affair.*

'Simone, I am heading off to my exercise class with

Scott. Call me if your dad makes any contact. I will be back at ten. See you later sweetie.'

I sat nervously in the Merc, the car seemed so conspicuous against the crumbling buildings and industrial ruin. This was the place that Ilderton had told me to go to. Rothesay dock in Clydebank on the edge of Glasgow had seen better times. Overgrown and abandoned railway tracks merged into the litter-strewn bushes and rusting fences. I could see the billboards he had told me about. It was behind the third one, *you cannot miss it, it advertises the new Supermarket they hope to build there next year.* I was annoyed at having to wait until the following morning to pick up the gun. I could still make it to Bendrennon before nightfall if I put my foot down.

Now look, I had better explain something here. I know you are thinking, *what the fuck is he going to do with a gun?* The honest answer is, I have no fucking idea. The words just seemed to come to me when I met Charlie boy and before you know it the deal was agreed. Of course, I am not a fucking madman. I had absolutely no intention of using it. Do you really think I was going to shoot Roni? Yes, great idea. I am already running from one possible murder, no way I was going to get away with another one. It was just to frighten her, maybe I would never need it, but somehow it just seemed right to get one. Maybe I am going fucking crazy.

I must admit, I was really impressed with Charles Cameron Ilderton. Obviously, there was more to the man than I first thought. He told me he could organise getting me a firearm but not until the following morning. His contact in Glasgow would place it in a plastic bag behind the third billboard. I was to pick it up no earlier than 8am. Charlie boy had warned me that if I was caught with it then any mention of him or his contact would make me a marked man. I think he knew I only wanted the firearm for show, and I promised him it would be ditched in the sea within a few days.

Christ, I felt like a nervous wreck scrambling through bushes looking for a plastic bag at five past eight in the morning. On the other side of the billboards, I could hear the occasional car or lorry drive past. The problem was, there was crap everywhere. Bottles, sweet wrappers and empty cans of lager lay strewn amongst the weeds and ruin. I spotted what I was looking for, *Bloody hell found it*. Before retreating to the car, I checked the contents inside the bag. Whatever it was, it had been dead for a long time. I threw the carrier away with disgust and was about to give up when I saw what I had come for. It was neatly wrapped and had obviously been placed in position. Within seconds I was back in the car and getting the hell out of Clydebank.

Charles Cameron Ilderton puffed away on his cigarette as he sat watching from his battered old Ford Sierra. Just a few hundred yards down the road he could make out the nervous figure of his client Matt Cunningham as he emerged from behind the billboards holding the plastic bag. This guy was going to be his golden ticket. *Twenty-five thousand fucking lovely pounds for a gun and another twenty-five grand for sitting about doing nothing. This is a dream come true, Charlie boy, a dream come fucking true.* Ilderton did not have any contacts who could get him a gun. That had just been a story to impress his client. The firearm had belonged to his father and had lain hidden in a drawer since just after the Second World War. He doubted if it still worked or if the bullets, he had supplied were even real. He had driven up earlier that morning and hidden the bag behind the billboard. All part of his little act to impress Cunningham. The truth was Charles Cameron Ilderton had very few clients anymore. He preferred drinking to working these days and hated every minute of his job. He was sick to death of sitting in a freezing car trying to take pictures of married men supposedly having an affair. *The work and money being offered by Cunningham would be enough to let him call it a day. Maybe, I can get more out of him? He must be fucking rolling in it if he can pay me 50 grand to do so little.*

The sharp tone of his mobile buzzing made Charlie jump. It could only be Cunningham as he had muted everyone else as agreed.

'Charlie, it's Matt here. Your man came good as promised. I got the gun just a few minutes ago.'

'That is excellent Matt, excellent. Just to let you know, I only made 5k out of the deal. He wanted 20k for it, more expensive than I had hoped, but you cannot barter with these guys. They are not the type you would want to cross. Guns are not easy to get. He had to import this one from, well let us just say it has seen action. Seen plenty of action Matt, plenty. I don't want to give too much away but, well let us just say the word Belfast. Belfast, Matt, Belfast.'

'Ok, Charlie. I will make up the difference for you at the end of the two weeks. Anyway, listen, I have another wee job that I need you to do.'

'Ok, Matt, yes what is it. Don't tell me you want a tank or a Spitfire now?' I ignored his joke. I was learning it was

best to filter out whatever he said and just tell him what I wanted.

'My wife Cara. She is having an affair. I need you to get me proof. His name is Scott, he works at Redbank Fitness studios in Newton Mearns. Can you do that for me?'

'Yes, Matt, should be an easy one. Leave it with me and I will call you when I have the evidence. That is my territory, Newton Mearns. It is a hotbed of extramarital affairs, a volcano of clandestine meetings between the married and the soon to be married.'

'Charlie, Charlie, Stop talking and listen will you.' Charlie sighed at the thought that his supposed retirement had lasted just ten fucking minutes. Back to sitting in a freezing car taking pictures, but at least the money was good.

'I am on my way to Bendrennon to find Roni Paterson. If I get things sorted out with her this evening, then hopefully I can be back tomorrow. Get started on the Cara thing straight away.' The phone clicked off. The curt tone made it quite clear to Charlie that he was the hired hand. It was dawning on him that Matt Cunningham was a man who gave out orders and expected them to be completed quickly and efficiently. He started the old Ford up and headed back towards the affluent Glasgow suburb of Newton Mearns, the supposed hotbed of extramarital affairs.

It must have been around four in the morning. I had covered the 280 miles as quickly as possible, lost in my imagination. I thought about Roni. The odd thing was even though I did not want to admit it, I was looking forward to seeing her again. I tried to visualise this picture of her looking old and haggard, like one of those witches in Hamlet. Stirring a pot of stew with one hand while she swigged a bottle of vodka with the other. But the vision of her when we were in love and she was young kept getting in the way.

I just knew I had to get there fast and confront her. Pay whatever she wanted and get back to normality. Ditch the gun in the sea, settle up with Charlie boy and then try and sort my marriage out. It was strange because challenging Cara once I had the evidence was the part that I feared doing the most. The other two I could fix with cash, it always worked. The trouble with money was as the Beatles once quoted, it can't buy you, love.

It was pitch black and the single-track road just north of Kinlochbervie twisted like a bastard. That is the thing about driving in Scotland. The further North you go, the less traffic there is. It is fine until you meet one of the locals, they know every bend and drive like fucking maniacs. You either give way or you die.

The Merc was hopeless for this kind of terrain, well that was my excuse. The reality was, I was looking at my phone. It was mounted on the dash, I had ignored everything except texts from Charlie. The number caught my eye, no name attached to it. I pressed the little screen and read the message. I was transfixed, looking at it in disbelief. It was one of those moments when you are so distracted that you forget you are driving. Most of the time you will look up and think, *Christ I don't remember looking at the road for the last two minutes*. Only this time I genuinely had not been looking at the road. Too fucking late, the Merc ignored the bend and went straight on. All I recall was endless branches battering the windscreen until it caved in around me. My foot slammed the brake pedal hard to the floor, but the wheels were already airborne. Something black flew towards me like a rocket and smacked me hard in the face. My brain made the decision that it might be best to disconnect from the world for the time being. Maybe it had decided to disconnect for good. No, I was not going to be that lucky.

(Possible Extract from 1970s
School reports at the age of 13)

Matt Cunningham- If he can channel his energy in the correct manner Matt has promise. Unfortunately, he seeks out the wrong company and can easily be led astray. This boy will either grow up to run his own successful business or end up in jail. I might as well flip a coin to try and guess which way he will go. Matt only listens to those he wants to hear.

Roni Paterson- A sweet girl but something dark lurks behind the smile. I sometimes wonder if she is borderline psychotic. She seems to be searching for something that is not there. Roni has already been sent home and barred for a few weeks from school. One occasion involved being drunk when she was 12 and the other was for damaging school property. A train wreck waiting to happen.

Charles Cameron Ilderton- This boy is just downright lazy. If he can find a scheme to give him an easy life, he will jump at it. Charlie is a nice boy, but he lacks any real potential. He struggles to concentrate on the simplest of tasks and talks too much. He is a daydreamer, wants to be a detective or a secret agent. I reckon he will be lucky to get a job emptying bins.

Cara Willis (Cunningham)- Well liked by all in her class. The sort of girl who will settle down and run a family. Solid as a rock and very smart as well. She is an integral part of the school netball team and has won various girls swimming medals. I could see her being a major success and making it to the upper echelons of the ladies' jobs market. Maybe a secretary, hairdresser or at a stretch an air hostess.

CHAPTER FOUR:
THE HOUSE AT THE
END OF THE WORLD

(2014)

Did you know that when airbags deploy in a car, they give off a sort of smoky gas that smells of burning? It can be quite disconcerting as it tends to make you think, *Jesus the car is on fire*. It wasn't but I thought it worthwhile mentioning it just in case you too decide to follow my example and take a shortcut through a field. The airbags also inflate and then deflate so you are left looking at something that resembles a crumpled white crisp packet. A family sized bag though, not one of those small packets you buy for a snack. I always imagined that the airbags would surround you like a soft comfy blanket while you plough through a field. They bloody well should do considering how much the Merc cost me. Anyway, I digress, the car was fucked.

We had come to rest about 100 yards from the road

having taken out a small stone wall and a hedge. I could feel my forehead was damp but other than that I seemed to be in one piece. Before trying to get out of the car I had another look at the phone. The message still shone brightly, each letter burning a hole through my brain.

Maybe I will just tell the Police so I can enjoy watching your demise, Cunningham. V

The car door opened without any problem and I stepped out onto the grassy moorland and the driving rain. The early winter darkness had set in and the rear lights of the Merc shone back towards the road. *Bastard*, within seconds my feet had sunk into the bog and I tumbled over into the mud. I looked up to see car headlights pulling up beside the hole the Merc had made in the little hedge. Suddenly blue strobe lights started dancing across the scene, reflecting and bouncing off the forlorn wreckage of my car.

'Hello, are you ok? I am coming down, stay where you are for now until I can get there.' I was still flat on my back in the mud. Maybe he thought I was dead or missing a few limbs. How lucky was that? The police passing by in the middle of nowhere just when I needed them. Had I called on my phone it would probably have taken hours for them to show up, if they came at all. I scrambled to my feet.

'It is ok, I think I am all right. Not sure about the car though, it might need more than a run through the car wash.' The policeman was squelching through the mud towards me, the blinding flash of his torch illuminating the scene around me. I was right, the car really did look fucked. And then it suddenly dawned on me, *the gun, the fucking gun. What if he finds it? Even if he doesn't then the recovery people will. Shit, I need to get the gun and hide it.* Too late, he was standing beside me.

'Christ, you are one lucky guy. I am amazed you are still in one piece. I think your car is in a bad way though. You look like you have cut your forehead, let's get you back to my vehicle.' I stared at him like an idiot, I was still thinking about the gun. And then I noticed something odd, did Highland policemen wear green uniforms? He was a paramedic; my luck had turned.

'I thought you must be the police, bloody hell how lucky can you get. You are the first one to drive past after I came off the road?'

'Maybe for you mate, not for me. I was out at one of the cottages, my last call of the day. I was heading back to Kinlochbervie as my shift was finished. You are incredibly lucky as the chances of anyone passing along this road are remote.'

David turned out to be a nice guy. The cut on my face was no more than a few scratches and other than that I seemed fine. He wanted me to go back to the village medical centre with him and get checked out, but I was having none of it. Time was against me, I had to get to that bitches' cottage and sort her out. *How the hell had she got hold of my phone number?* There was no point in replying, I was looking forward to seeing her face when I knocked on the door of her hovel.

'You will need to report the accident to the police and arrange for the car to be picked up. Where exactly are you going? There are very few houses around this area.' I could tell that David knew there was something odd about a stranger being out here in the middle of winter.

'I am on my way to visit an old friend of mine. Roni Paterson, she lives at Bendrennon cottage. Do you know her by any chance? Is it far, could I walk?' David looked at me as though I was crazy.

'Yes, I know her, it is about three miles further on up the road and then about another mile up a dirt track. Look I will run you up, but she will wonder what the hell has happened, you are covered in mud and your face looks a bit worse for wear.' I lifted the boot of the car up and discretely placed the plastic bag with the gun into my travel case before trudging back through the field with my rescuer. Within minutes David was heading back the way he had just come to drop me off at Bendrennon cottage. I lifted my mobile and called Charlie boy, this guy was turning out to be a Godsend. A fucking expensive one but a Godsend none the less.

'Charlie, it is Matt, I need you...' As usual, he started answering me before I had even asked a question.

'Hi Matt, yes I am on the job. Nothing so far. Cara went to the gym a few hours ago but is still in there. She is with Scott, but it is a class so nothing untoward yet. Unless it is a group orgy, hahahaha.'

'Charlie, shut the fuck up and listen to me. Forget the Cara thing for now. I need you to contact the police in Sutherland and tell them I crashed my car. I also need you to organise getting it picked up, see if it is a write off or not. I think it will be. I will text you the exact location, the registration is Matt 1.'

'Bloody Jesus in a handbag Matt. Are you ok, you don't do things by half? Yes, yes, I will get on it. Erm, just one thing.' I was becoming aware that Charlie was not slow when it came to adding on extra costs.

'Charlie, I will cover whatever it costs, it won't come out of your fee. Look, I do not have time now to piss around talking about money. Just do everything I ask over the next two weeks and I will pay you 50k plus any extra expenses. In fact, I will pay you whatever you fucking want, just get on with it.'

'Your wish is my command boss. Your wish is my command. I am on the case at this very moment. Well maybe not this actual moment but I soon will be. If you know what I mean?' I could sense his joy at the money I was offering to throw at him, it was shining through in the excitement of his voice.

'Oh, and Charlie. Once you get the Merc sorted out, get back onto the Cara affair thing. It should be easy to prove, she is never away from him. I need to go, I will be in touch. Don't fuck up, get the car out of the field, do you understand?' I cut him off before he could reply. I did not have the time or energy to listen to his endless gibbering. It was only then that it dawned on me that David had been listening to every word of my conversation.

'I know it all sounds a bit odd David. The chap I was talking to is a private eye. He is helping me with my potential divorce case. I decided to come up and see my long-time friend Roni, she is great at giving me advice.' He looked at me and nodded. He was not daft, who the hell paid someone 50k to take a few photographs?

Charles Cameron Ilderton was sitting inside his car watching the well-heeled woman coming in and out of Redbank fitness studios in the affluent Glasgow suburb of Newton Mearns. He was enjoying working for Matt, this was the excitement he needed. *This guy Cunningham is rich and crazy, a right fucking madman. Guns, money, crashed cars and strange women. What more could I ask for?* And yet even though he was enjoying the fun he somehow sensed that it was not just his client who might be heading for disaster, it could be him as well. For now, the money more than made up for it.

Charlie had switched between various jobs all his life, but he had always ended up coming back to private investigation work. It was the only thing he really knew how to do. But even being a detective had proved to be boring and low paid. Like many who keep working in their sixties, Charlie hated his job. It did not help that he had hardly saved anything into his pension. Most of his free cash had been spent on drinking and having a good time. Maybe, just maybe, he had been thrown a lifeline. Ok, 50,000 was not going to buy him a holiday home in the Bahamas but with a bit of luck, he might be able to get more money out of Matt Cunningham. *Just do everything he asks you, Charlie, while looking for opportunities to screw more cash out of him.* He picked up his tablet and started to search for the phone number of the local police in Kinlochbervie.

David's car was one of those fast response units rather than an ambulance. Inside it smelled of disinfectant, it reminded me of a hospital waiting room. I washed my face with wet wipes, but I had to admit I looked a mess. I was filthy after the fall into the bog but cared not a jot. I was just looking forward to seeing Roni's face when I appeared out of the night and ruined her game.

'So, David you mentioned you know my mate, Roni. I have not seen her face to face for several years. We just keep in touch by email, how is she?'

'Miss Paterson. Yes, she is fine.' I could see he was keeping something back, so I tried to push him for more information. That is the problem with these professional medical types, everything is a bloody secret.

'I know she went through a tough time for a while. She is a good mate, I am so looking forward to seeing her again.' It was no good though, David was not biting but it was obvious he was hiding what he really thought of her.

The car pulled up at the edge of a rickety looking wooden gate that barred entrance to a dirt track. The headlights picked out the winding little path heading up into the dark treeless moorland.

'This is it, Matt. I must admit I am not comfortable leaving you here. I am happy to drive up to her cottage if you want, you are going to get soaked. You really should have come back to Kinlochbervie and got yourself checked out.'

'No, it is ok David, you have done more than enough already. I really appreciate it mate. You take care now. I will just jump out and walk from here. In fact, I will give Roni a call, I am sure she will come down to meet me.' David turned in the driver seat and looked at me.

'Look, Matt, you seem like a nice guy but, well something does not make sense. Take care of yourself up there.' His comment had not only taken me by surprise, but it had unnerved me as well.

'What do you mean, David?'

'Well, Look, I know It is none of my business and I am only giving my opinion as a local rather than a professional medic.' He turned the car engine off as though to give added impact to what was coming next. He needn't have bothered, by now I was starting to feel like I was about to walk into a horror movie.

'Miss Paterson, or Roni as you know her. Well, she only appeared around here a few years ago. She purchased Bendrennon Cottage after it had been lying empty for several years. She must have got it for next to nothing as it was falling to bits, still is if I remember. Anyway, just be careful. I don't know what your relationship is with her or how long since you have seen her but, well. Let us just say she has had a few run-ins with the locals including the police.' I tried to bluff that I knew more about her current situation than I did.

'Oh yes, I know. Roni told me all about the problems she was having. I suppose it is because she is an outsider and, well you know?' David turned and looked at me in surprise.

'Know what?'

'Well she is an alcoholic, everyone is aware of it. I think that is her main problem.' David looked confused.

'I take it you have not spoken to her in a while then? I know for a fact that she has not had a drink in the last year. Tea total as far as I understand.' I could tell he was now feeling unsure about my motive for visiting Bendrennon. I had to think fast.

'Look, David. I am going, to be honest with you. Me and Miss Paterson used to be a couple when we were younger. We stayed close friends over the years, but I have not been in touch since she moved up North. This is a surprise visit, but I know she will be happy to see me. I have helped her out financially over the years.' Christ, I was becoming good at lying, what was happening to me?

David seemed to relax and smiled at me.

'I have to be honest with you Matt. I knew you could not be telling the truth about talking to Miss Paterson recently.' I laughed to try and keep things light-hearted even though I did not feel that way.

'How did you know I was not telling the truth?' He was laughing now. The joke was on me.

'It was the bit you mentioned about sending her an email.' Before I could ask him to explain he made it obvious that he needed to go.

'Well good luck whatever you find up there Matt.' He leaned over and pulled the door handle on my side.

'I need to rush; the misses will be wondering what has happened to me.'

I stepped out of the car and waved goodbye to my

knight in shining armour, well a knight in a green uniform then, before heading out up the lonely dark track. One bleak mile and I could, at last, confront the guilt of my past. At least now I could be certain that Roni and V had to be the same blackmailer. From what David had told me about her involvement with the Police it was obvious that she was a nut job. But one thing unsettled me. The news that she was no longer drinking ruined the story I had invented about her. The reason she was trying to blackmail me was that she was an alcoholic. She had no control over her life, booze was everything. If she had stopped drinking, then it meant her blackmail had a cunning and devious side to it. Somehow that did not fit with the Roni I had known.

As the car headlights disappeared into the distance I stopped and opened my travel bag. And do you know what I did? Yes, like some sort of Wild West lunatic I took out the little gun and placed it inside my coat. It was only when I looked up that I noticed the little handwritten sign attached to the wooden gate. I got as close as possible so I could read it in the dark. This was getting bizarre.

Welcome to Bendrennon. Beware of Roni Paterson.

It was only on further inspection that I worked out that the last four words had been added on by hand. It looked like my blackmailer had made an impression on the locals. My fingers wrapped around the little gun inside my coat. You can call me a big coward if you want, but it made me feel better.

The track was no wider than one car and even that would have been a stretch. It climbed slowly up the steep moorland. The only shelter from the wind and rain was the occasional stone wall or hedge. My eyes became adjusted to the darkness but even that still only allowed me to see a few yards ahead. I thought about the events of the last few days. How life had changed. I wondered how the hell things could have gone so quickly from looking forward to early retirement to chasing up crazy bitches in the middle of fucking nowhere. And yet you know what? The funny thing was I had enjoyed my little roller coaster ride, but now it had to end. She had to stop, I wanted to get back home and sort things out with Cara. Show her the proof of her affair and take things forward from there.

I had been walking with my head bowed, lost in my thoughts when I suddenly became aware of a change to my surroundings. The road had levelled out and was now sheltered by crumbling stone walls and sickly-looking trees. A few more steps in the oozing mud let the path take me to a rotting wooden gate. It leaned at an angle and was only held up by a piece of rope attached to a post. I peered through the gloom at the damp walls of Bendrennon Cottage. It was a dilapidated single-story building surrounded by various bits of junk including metal tins and various moulding plant pots. There was no sign of a car or any kind of light. As quietly as possible I climbed over the gate and edged up to the front door. Wind chimes hung over the entrance adding a ghostly jangling sound to what already looked like a set from one of those old Hammer Horror films. It was only now as I stood at the door that I realised how ridiculous this whole situation was. I had charged up North, crashing cars and hitching lifts without any thought about how I would approach things when I arrived. I could hardly knock politely on the door and say, *Hi Roni, you have not changed one bit in 35 years. It is me, Matt, your old accomplice. How the fuck are you old girl. Anyway, to the point. How much do you want from me to get out of my life you fucking fruitcake? Oh, and by the way, just in case you think I am kidding, I have a gun with me.*

I decided the best way forward was to check the place out and think of a plan. It did seem strange that there was no car around, maybe she was away somewhere. I edged around the side and then the back of the house. One thing is for sure, I would make a crap housebreaker. Within seconds I had tripped over an old wheelbarrow and made enough noise to wake the dead. I jumped up, more mud on my nice jacket. This was becoming a habit. I reached out in the dark to grab hold of the fence and my fingers touched something warm. *Oh, for fuck sake*, I let out a shriek that nearly gave both me and the poor goat a heart attack. The bloody thing was tethered to an old wooden fence surrounding the cottage and I had frightened the living crap out of it. The poor creature went crazy trying to get away, but the rope held it firmly. I moved forward to try and calm it down but that just caused the terrified animal to panic even more. With an almighty cracking sound, the wood gave way and the goat went running off into the dark pulling the rope and part of the fence along with it.

I sat down, perspiration running down my forehead and my heart pounding like a bastard in my chest. *Fuck this,* I thought. *Why am I pissing around, she is the one who is trying to screw me? Knock the fucking door you idiot and get this over with. Christ, she might even make me a cup of tea once I give her the money she is after.* I trudged with imagined assurance back to the front door and rattled it loudly.

Nothing, no light came on, no shouts of *who the fuck is it*, nothing. I was starting to panic, *what if she no longer lived here and had left, making sure to keep one step ahead of me?* I grabbed the handle in frustration and was stunned when the door simply opened in front of me. *Of course, who would lock a door around here?* It really was the house at the end of the world. I stepped inside and stood in the dark hallway.

Somehow, I had expected the place to smell damp, feel unloved but the sweet scent of patchouli oil rose in my nostrils. My hand felt along the wall for a light switch but if there was one, I could not find it. It was becoming obvious that no one was in. At the end of the hall, I found a small table with a large ornate candle holder. Beside it lay a box of matches! A fucking box of matches, *Jesus, who the hell uses matches these days?* I suppose that is the trouble when you have spent years being cosseted by an affluent city lifestyle working for a high-tech company. It dawned on me that the place had no electricity. Doubts were beginning to creep into my head again, how could V and the hermit Roni be the same person? Now I understood why David had laughed when I said I had emailed Roni. This place looked as though the internet or even a phone signal would be considered a luxury. The candles flickered into life and I set out to search for the secrets of Bendrennon Cottage.

The hallway led off into five more rooms, a small living area adjoined an even smaller kitchen. The remaining three rooms being a bathroom, what had maybe been a tiny bedroom but was now a junk store and another larger bedroom. The place was a clutter of candle holders, ornaments, indoor plant pots, ornate rugs, and cushions. Somehow, I had expected to find dirt and squalor, instead, the place had a homely feel. It obviously belonged to a woman and someone you would consider a hippy or new age. I don't know why I left the bedroom until last, it just felt so intrusive to go in there. Slowly I edged the door open, *Christ, what if she is in here asleep, maybe she wears a hearing aid and it is switched off?* It would fucking need to be the way I crashed about like a bloody great elephant. But I did not have to worry. The bed was neatly made, a flowery throw and endless patterned cushions rounded off by three or four teddy bears. Teddy Fucking bears!

I had expected to find tables littered with cuttings and photographs of me. Computer screens with half-full ashtrays and empty gin bottles scattered everywhere. But there was nothing incriminating to be found. No electricity and an occupant who was tea total, this did not fit in at all. It all looked so cute, a little country cottage owned by an aging female recluse.

I had to find something or get the hell out of there. The place looked lived in, she would be coming back for sure. Opening every drawer or cupboard revealed nothing to link Roni and our past together. Old bills, pamphlets, cards, books, even a few old photographs of Roni and her mum from years ago. Not a single drop of alcohol could be found anywhere, no empty bottles never mind full ones. David had been telling the truth that was for sure. I glanced up at the wall and for the first time, it registered with me that canvass paintings covered each space. Closer scrutiny revealed the name Roni Paterson signed at the bottom of each one. Sea views, mountains, and distant lighthouses. Fuck, this was just too ordinary. *How could this be the home of a blackmailer, it was impossible. Christ the place did not even have fucking electricity.*

But God moves in mysterious ways as my old Auntie Annie used to say. Well, she didn't really as I don't have an Auntie Annie, but you know what I mean. I don't know why but my eyes moved across to the chair sitting in front of the unlit fire. And there it was, a little writing table with one of those drawers that slide underneath. I just knew I had found what I was looking for and boy was it good timing because unbeknown to me a car was slowing down to take the dirt road and climb the last mile to Bendrennon Cottage.

I slid the drawer open and found more bills and old letters. But it was the one that sat at the top of the pile that my hand lifted. Only a few words were scrawled across the little piece of paper but these few letters where enough to make me smile. *Got you now you swindling bitch.* All my doubts had gone, I would wait here as long as it took until she returned. Two things hidden in my coat pocket gave me the key to getting my life back to normal. The gun to frighten the shit out of her and my cheque book to buy her silence. I doubted it would cost much to pay her off, well she was supposed to be a hippy after all. Give her enough to buy some more incense candles and cushions and the bitch could go back to painting lighthouses. And the damning words that were no doubt intended to be the next note I would receive?

A murderer must always pay the price in the long run. V

The sound of a car could be heard climbing the track in the distance. I could just make out headlights coming up the hill towards the cottage, she was home. How fucking appropriate that she would return just at that moment.

I blew the candle out and sat in her chair, holding the incriminating piece of paper. I will admit I felt pleased with myself, but I won't kid you that I was feeling calm. I was scared, I had this picture of Roni looking like a haggard old witch, long grey hair covering her blotched wrinkly evil face. Thirty-five years or more since I had last seen her, she had gone down while I had gone up. How dare she try to ruin me, she was as big a culprit as I was. Maybe if she had not been such a thieving kleptomaniac then we could have gone our separate ways and never met again. My other hand reached into my coat pocket to place the gun beside me just as the sound of a car door slamming filtered into the dark sitting room.

I listened to her footsteps crunching across the muddy track and assumed she was walking towards the cottage. For some reason it then went silent, by now I was shitting myself. *What if somehow, she sensed I was here, maybe she had a fucking gun as well? Christ calm down Matt you bloody big wimp.* I heard the car boot lid slam shut. That explained the delay, she was collecting something. More steps and then the front door opened. I heard her place something on the floor and then strike a match as she lit some candles. My heart was pounding like a bastard. It was no use, I could not sit in the chair pretending I was James Bond. I jumped up and shouted, 'Roni, it's me, Matt. Matt Cunningham. Don't panic, I let myself in when I found the door unlocked.' I stood up to face her with the gun in my hand.

Silence followed but I could see she was standing beside the living room door holding the candle as the light flickered underneath the gap at the bottom. Slowly the door opened and there she stood, silhouetted by the candlelight. Standing facing me was Roni Paterson, once my ally, once my lover, now my nightmare.

'I expected you to come looking for me, Matt. Maybe not to break into my home but I did expect you none the less.'

The short black hair was gone, replaced by a mix of blonde and grey cascading over her shoulders in curls. It was still her face but now lined with the march of time. She wore one of those long summer dresses even though it was mid-winter. An oversized farmers coat and knitted gloves completed the ensemble. On her feet, she wore pink Wellington boots while in her hands, she held a large ornate flower pot. We stared at each other, I wanted to hate her but could not find it in me. I had expected her to look like an evil witch, but it was still the same slim Roni with the pretty but much older face. She looked small and ghostly with the candlelight adding a yellow glow to her face.

'Why have you got a gun in your hand Matt? Are you fucking serious? I thought you might have brought me flowers instead.' She threw her head back and laughed.

'Oh right, I get it now. You have come here to shoot me.' The words were said without any malice or mocking but it was enough to snap me to my senses.

'You know damn fucking well why I am here Roni, or should I call you fucking V? Just tell me how much you want and then I can get the fuck out of here.' The expression on her face changed to one of surprise and then anger. 'What on earth are you talking about Cunningham. You break into my fucking house and then start throwing accusations around. What the hell are you on about?'

'Don't fuck with me, Roni. I know damn well you are trying to blackmail me. I have the fucking proof here in my hand you scheming bitch.'

I threw the piece of paper down at her feet. She slowly bent down and picked it up, while still holding the plant pot. She then calmly walked towards me and placed the container down on the little table before pulling the drawer open. Her hands rummaged around amongst the paperwork before she pulled out a ripped envelope. Roni moved within inches of my face and threw the piece of paper on the floor.

'That is the envelope that came a few days ago. Inside it was the letter from whoever the fuck V is. They are not just after you, it is both of us, you fucking idiot.'

I picked up the letter with the words scrawled across it. What a fool I had been. Why would Roni write a letter to herself, it had to be someone else? I read the words again.

A murderer must always pay the price in the long run. V

My ordered world was collapsing again, just like the time I had seen the words written on that first note. The rushed conclusion had suited me because money would sort it all out. I would place the jigsaw piece with the pound sign on it perfectly into position and walk away. The realisation that my blackmailer was still unknown brought the threatening words in the phone text back to life.

Maybe I will just tell the police so I can enjoy watching your demise, Cunningham. V

My head spun in turmoil, not only was I completely wrong, my erroneous assumption had now alienated my only ally in this complete fucking mess. Roni was talking again but it was as though the words were floating in the air making no sense at all.

'I was waiting for you to find me, Matt. I knew it was a blackmail note and that you would eventually turn up. Whoever it is won't get anything from me. Look around you, I have nothing. I had heard you had made your fortune. I reckon it is you they really want.' I tried to regain some composure even though I still felt like an idiot. For some reason, I was still holding the bloody gun in my hand.

'I am sorry Roni, I am confused. I just assumed it was you.' She ignored my rambling and continued speaking.

'And to think I was feeling excited about seeing you again after all these years. Typical bloody man, everything is always my fault.' She was talking as though we had only parted five minutes ago.

How are you anyway, Matt? It is nice to see you again even if you are here to shoot me.' She seemed to be totally unphased by the man opposite her holding the gun as she walked calmly back towards the little table.

I stood there dumbstruck, wondering what I could possibly say to get out of the situation. And do you know what the only fucking thing I managed to come up with was?'Roni, I think I might have given your pet goat a heart attack. It ran off with the fence still attached to it. I will give you the money to repair the damage, I promise.'

Roni looked at me for a few seconds and I swear she was about to laugh. Maybe that was just to side-track me though as she calmly picked up the plant pot again. I could see her hands moving but it still did not register what was coming next. She was always more of a punk than me, she had the real attitude and spirit. I was just a fraud, I just played at it. The container came crashing down on my head and I crumbled to the floor while still holding the gun.

What the fuck had happened to my easy retirement? I was being blackmailed by someone called V who might not exist, my marriage was in a mess and ...oh yes... I had just lost a fight with a small woman and a plant pot despite being armed. Maybe if I had been conscious, I could have consoled myself with the words, *well it can only get better from here Matt*. But you know what? Thank the fucking lord I was out cold because things were not going to get any better. They were about to get a whole lot fucking worse, trust me.

(Northern Time's newspaper cutting. 2013)

Miss Roni Paterson of Bendrennon Cottage, Kinlochbervie appeared at Tain Sheriff court this week charged with affray and breach of the peace. Paterson pled guilty to assaulting local man Kenneth Tyler after an altercation in the Coulter Bar around 4pm last Tuesday. It was alleged that both Tyler and Paterson had been drinking all day and had an argument while playing a game of pool. Barman, Jamie Forsyth alleged that Paterson called Tyler *a dirty cheating Sheep shagger* before striking him with a pool Que.

Paterson had claimed that she acted in self-defence after Mr. Tyler told her, *I reckon that feckin goat you keep up at Bendrennon is a better pool player than you, Roni.* Barman Jamie Forsyth and another two witnesses present on the day of the incident confirmed that Mr. Tyler had done nothing wrong other than pot a winning black in the top left-hand corner of the table. To laughter in the court, Mr. Forsyth commented, 'It was feck all tae di wi Kenny da'in fuck all. It was that Maddie Paterson, she disnae like tae get beat that's aw. She fair smacked him ower the heid when he sank the black. Everywan knows she should be in a feckin looney bin.'

Paterson admitted that she had a drinking problem during sentencing. It was also noted that she had previous convictions both in the UK and had served a prison sentence in Italy. When asked by Judge Brendon O'Callaghan if she had anything to say, Miss Paterson replied, 'Aye, it will be the last time I will play that dirty cheating bastard Tyler at pool again.' When asked to maintain order and respect, the defendant apologised and said she had been tea total since the incident some months ago and had been getting addiction counselling as well as pool lessons.

Judge O'Callaghan shook his head before fining Miss Paterson £100 and bound her over to keep the peace.

CHAPTER FIVE:
DREAM CAR VERSUS
THE TIN SNAIL

(2014)

The room flickered with a dim yellow light dancing amongst the shadows. My eyes tried desperately to adjust as my brain attempted to make sense of the confusion. I was stretched out on the floor with my head supported by pillows and my body covered by a patterned blanket. Opposite me, I could make out flames gyrating in the fireplace while candles burned all around the room. It reminded me of a Christmas card scene, but something was wrong. Oh yes, that was it. My head throbbed with pain. A blurred image moved at the edge of my vision, and I turned slowly to see what it was. She was kneeling beside me dabbing a wet cloth against my head while holding one of my hands. So much for the vision of Roni as one of Hamlet's witches.

'I am sorry Matt, but what was I supposed to do? I have not seen you since I was a teenager and you did break into my home with a gun.' *I wanted to reply, the fucking door was open, is that the same as breaking in?* The words would not come though and slowly I drifted back into the world of hazy dreams. Maybe I needed that belt across the head because I had the best sleep since V had first reminded me that I was a murderer. I would not stir again until the cold morning started to infiltrate the blanket and the fire lay dead in the hearth.

It was nearly mid-day and we sat opposite each other at the kitchen table. I had sent a message back to V asking what it was they wanted, telling them they could have whatever they required so long as it ended this whole sorry mess. No reply came. We called the number and it was disconnected. Whoever it was had complete control, they held all the power so long as their identity remained a mystery. I felt better than I had for some time, even though my head still hurt. Roni had plied me with sleeping pills, and I had been out for the count for twelve hours. I watched her pour me another cup of tea from the pot. She looked good despite the mess life had thrown her way. Maybe she could do with a session on one of those makeover programs but behind the mismatch of clothes, she was still pretty and slim. Even the mixture of blonde and grey curls tumbling down her sides added to the feminine touch. It would be a dangerous thing to underestimate Roni Paterson though, my head bore witness to that.

'The number they sent the text on is dead Roni.' Whoever is blackmailing us knows what they are doing.' She sat down at the table opposite me and lifted her teacup before replying.

'Ok, well we just have to assume that whoever it is will be in touch. There is no point in stressing Matt, they have us by the balls.' Roni laughed as she said the words. It irked me that she seemed to take all this as just something that happened. *Why worry, what will be will be.* I knew why, she had nothing to lose. Roni had been through so much worse than this. She could handle whatever shit the future could throw at her. For me it was different. I had always been in control, now I felt like a puppet dangling at the end of the strings of our blackmailer.

'That's the problem, Roni. I have already been away for almost four days. I promised Cara and my work that I would be back and in touch after one week. I cannot keep them all blocked on my phone for any longer than that.

Cara is not daft, she is already suspicious, she might even be worried enough to go to the Police. She probably thinks I have gone away to top myself.'

'I doubt it, Matt, you don't come across as someone who would commit suicide.'

'What makes you think that? You have not seen me in 30 odd years, since when did you become an expert on my life?' She laughed and leaned forward over the table.

'I know you well enough Matt Cunningham. You were always a coward and anyway, it was obvious that you would make it big one day. Be successful, become posh.' I knew she was trying to wind me up, but her comment irked me slightly.

'Fuck off Roni, I was a punk just the same as you. Anyway, at least I could play guitar, your singing was enough to frighten the dead.'

'You a punk? It was me who was the punk. You thought you were Eric fucking Clapton, except you were shit at playing the guitar. She laughed again but not mocking me, it was just the way Roni was. She called things as she saw them, no matter how blunt. Even though I was in deep trouble, it felt good to see her again. It was the same Roni, older and maybe wiser. But she could still make me smile.

'Anyway, continue with the story you were telling me, Roni. Why did you move to Italy and what happened?'

'I went over in the early nineties. I was in a mess in Kilmarnock, drinking too much and just screwing around. I was desperate for a change and just grasped at whatever came my way. Anyway, to cut a long story short, I managed to wangle a job with a nice family in Italy teaching their kids English.'

'English! For fuck sake Roni, did they not realise you came from Kilmarnock?' She ignored me and continued.

'Anyway, as usual, I messed things up. I Met a guy and moved to a small hillside town called Campana in the Cosenza region of Southern Italy. Things went downhill from there. He was a drinker and even though I tried, so was I. I got into trouble, did some time in jail there before being sent back.' Roni made it plain this was the end of the life story as she went quiet and started clearing the kitchen. Moving pots and flowers around into a vaguely organised chaos of mismatched colours.

'What did you do time for? I mean was it for a parking ticket or was it your usual nicking stuff from shops?' I was sorry I said it as soon as the words came out, but it was too late. We both recognised the irony of my joke.

'I don't want to talk about it, Matt. I came back to Scotland, stayed in Kilmarnock for a while. That was a bigger mistake than going to Italy turned out to be.' For the first time since I had met her again, she looked sad and tired.

'I Had some trouble in Kily, had to get away fast. I got this place with the little bit of money my mum left me after she died. I had a few problems here as well. But in the last year, I have really tried to get my life together. And then this fucking message and you turn up. I suppose I was never meant to get it easy.' She smiled as though she had composed herself again and continued to fuss around the kitchen while I sat cradling my cup of hot tea.

'Ok Roni, I understand. Look, back to the shit we are in. Did you ever tell anyone about what happened in Liverpool? I mean did you mention me and that day? It was strange how we would only talk about Birkby in vague references. As though mentioning his name was an admission of guilt. Afraid to be specific in case it was followed by a knock on the door and the Police. I continued talking.

'I have never once uttered a word about it. I blanked it all off, so it cannot be me.' Roni sighed and put down the tea towel she had just picked up.

'Look, Matt, I was an alcoholic for years. I cannot say

for sure, but I probably did mention it to people. Maybe, boyfriends, I had at the time. I don't know, but I probably did. Sorry.'

'Fuck sake Roni, so that narrows it down to the population of Italy and possibly Scotland. Any other countries you want to throw in for good measure?'

'Look, Cunningham, Let's not forget that it was you who tripped the shopkeeper up. Not me, I was just a bystander.'

'Oh yes, A bystander who had just robbed his shop and then fled with me after we left him for dead. Let's just say we will both end up in prison, the only difference is you will know how to handle it. I will probably spend my days getting bummed by murderers and junkies.' Roni sat opposite me and stared into my eyes. We stayed like that for a few minutes saying nothing but we both knew. The shame and guilt of leaving an innocent man to die had been with us since that day. I had just been better at keeping it hidden in a dark corner of my brain. Roni was a better person than me, she had punished herself every hour since year zero.

We both jumped in our seats, my phone buzzed with a message. It could only be V as everyone else except Ilderton was on mute and he would have called rather than text. It was a new number, they were always one step ahead. I read the words out to Roni.

I have decided what I want. It is time for you and your murdering accomplice to pay for what you did. Firstly, let me be clear, if you tell anybody or do not do exactly as I say, I will simply send your names and the details of the murder to the Police. Follow this instruction to the letter or face the consequences Cunningham. You will pay me in cash, I have yet to decide how much. I want you to go and get your old friend Roni Paterson. She lives at Bendrennon Cottage near Kinlochbervie. You must go now as I then want you to drive to Liverpool, both of you. Be there by 4 pm tomorrow when I will contact you again. V

In anger and frustration, I quickly typed a reply. *Why the hell should I let you tell me what to do. What proof do you have that I did anything? Who the fuck are you anyway? What does V mean?* I did not expect a response, so it was a surprise when the phone beeped once more. I wished I had not asked as now there could be no doubt. My last grasp at freedom, my final card played to get my life back.

Oh dear Mr. Cunningham, are we getting annoyed? Why, it was Mister Birkby. It was him you murdered after you both robbed his shop. The concert, how could you forget Social

Decline? What a great band, up there with the Stones and The Beatles. V means nothing, I am neither male or female, it should not matter to you. Liverpool at six tomorrow bring her or face the music. Oh, do you get the pun, face the music? I should be on the stage. Get moving you fucking murderer. V

I read the words to Roni and then tried to call back but as expected it was dead. They would simply use a new number or phone each time and then destroy it. But we had the first little advantage in the battle with our tormentor. I had outrun them by one full day. They obviously did not know I had already found Roni, it gave us a slight advantage. Well, it gave us a few more hours to think of a plan. I was already calling Charles Cameron Ilderton. As I pressed his name on my phone, I looked up to see Roni putting her coat on and rummaging about in one of the kitchen drawers. 'What are you doing Roni, are you going somewhere?'

'Not me, us, Matt. I have always wanted to go back to Liverpool. It is time for us to face up to the past. It is time for the road trip, the one we should have done years ago.'

I put my phone down and looked at her. And then it started to dawn on me. I had travelled the world on business, flight after flight, taxis, trains, hired cars, even buses. Mile upon mile of faceless journeying. Not once had they meant anything to me. But this drive from the tip of Scotland to Liverpool would be the only one that counted. This was it, no need for a return ticket. This would be one way. The road trip to hell, but then had that not always been our destination. We had been damned from the minute we walked into that store. There had never been any chance of escape. It had simply been a reprieve until judgement day.

Cara sat alone at the table. She had deliberately chosen the little coffee shop in Fenwick village so she would not be interrupted by anyone she knew. Eric Carter had never been her favourite person. She put up with him because he had been Matt's friend for a long time. It was not that she disliked him, it was because he seemed ill at ease around her. Almost as though he put up a defensive wall to protect himself. And, he was now divorced for the second time. No matter how fair-minded a person tried to be, twice divorced rang alarms bells.

The door rattled open causing the few people in the café to look around at the newcomer. Eric was still a handsome man even in his late fifties. Tall with cropped hair and the sort of figure that spoke of hours spent in the gym working out. He had a rugged look that both men and women admired, the opposite of Matt. Although Cara's husband took care of himself, he looked like the picture of middle-class normality. When it came to looks most would have said that Matt had married above his station. Cara was still tall and slim, she carried the elegant confidence that had been learned from her modelling days. She stood up to welcome Eric, the rugged athlete and the ex-model dressed in long black boots and tight jeans. You know what? Now that I come to think about it, they almost looked like the perfect couple.

'Hi Cara, you are looking amazing, as always. You must have been drunk when you agreed to marry wee Matt.' It was the usual forced humour from Eric, he could not help it when he was around Cara, just her presence intimidated him. It was not that he was being mean about his long-time friend, he would have said the same to his face. The couple sat for ten minutes and chatted about nothing in particular. Cara skirted around Eric's latest divorce, trying not to offend him or look like she was prying. They had to eventually get to the reason Cara had asked for the meeting. They both knew what was coming but the niceties must always be dispensed with first.

'Eric, I am worried about Matt. This disappearing for a week and turning his phone off. Do you have any idea what it is about, anything at all? He just left in such a rush, as though he had to get away as quickly as possible. Simone is worried sick and even his work colleagues have called to ask if he is ok.' Cara hated having to admit the failings in her marriage to Eric of all people. But she had no choice, something was wrong and the more she thought about it, the more she worried.

'He, he never really told me anything Cara, other than he felt crowded and needed solitude. I think it is maybe just the thought of retiring. All men go through this, Matt possibly more than others. After all, it was a stressful job. He had massive responsibilities, you do not just walk away from that without some impact.' Cara showed a rare edge of impatience, she wanted something to grasp onto rather than a lecture. She looked into Eric's eyes before he could avert them.

'Is Matt having an affair, Eric? I need to know.' Eric blushed, it was tough enough being around Cara but having to answer awkward questions as well!' He pushed his chair back and sighed before facing down his friend's wife.

'Look, Cara, as far as I know, he is not seeing anyone else. I don't know for sure, but I doubt it. Can I be honest with you on something?'

'Yes, yes, just tell me, Eric. I have this fear that time is running out and he might need help.'

'Well, ok. Matt thinks it is you who is having an affair. He thinks it is that guy who runs the exercise class, Is it Scott or something?'

'Oh, for fuck sake Eric. I have been over this with him many times before. I am not having an affair with Scott or anyone else for that matter. I do not understand why he thinks that. It is me and him that is the problem, no one else is involved.'

For the first time in his life, Eric felt like an equal to Cara. She seemed defeated and he felt sorry for her. She no longer looked like the perfect woman, just another human being finding life tough to cope with. At long last, he did not feel inadequate while in her presence. Eric leaned forward and touched Cara's hand to comfort her. Christ, they had known each other for years and finally, the barrier had come down. 'Maybe there is one thing, it might not mean anything, but it is all I have.' Cara looked up, she had been close to breaking down.

'Yes, go on, what is it, Eric?'

'Well, Matt called me a few days back. He was looking for the name of the Private Investigator I told him about a few years back. When I asked him what it was for, he seemed very evasive. Almost impatient, it was not like him. He said it was to check up on you but somehow, I got a feeling it was something else. Something worse, Fuck, I don't know Cara. I feel the same as you. I don't understand what is wrong with Matt or were the hell he has gone. I know the guy quite well; do you want me to check it out?' Cara stayed silent for a few seconds, something was telling her that this would be the key to finding out what was really going on with her estranged husband.

'That would be good Eric. I have nothing else to go on, he has disappeared off the face of the earth. I mean, even though Matt said he was taking a week out, I somehow expected to hear from him. Why would he cut all contact? I think he has blocked all numbers. Oh God Eric, what if something has happened to him.' Eric again tried to comfort Cara, as he clasped his hand over hers on the table. It might have signalled a coming together of the two long-time adversaries. Maybe Cara was beginning to think that Eric was not so aloof after all. The twice-married friend of her missing husband who always seemed to keep her at arm's length. There was no maybe for Eric though. He would never admit it to himself, but he had always wanted Cara.

He had no choice but to treat her as the enemy because he was scared, he would cross the line. She was the one woman he knew he could never have. But she had let her armour down and now the boundaries were becoming blurred.

'I will call him on the way home Cara and get back to you straight away.' They walked out of the coffee shop together and had a friendly farewell embrace before heading in different directions to their cars.

The old Ford Mondeo was parked discretely on the other side of the road. The tinted windows gave little hint of the large man sitting inside it with his camera pointed at the departing couple.

I squelched out of the cottage through the wet mud and damp rain. Roni followed behind me carrying a plastic shopping bag. We had time on our hands if V did not expect us to get to Liverpool until six pm the following day. I dragged my now battered suitcase behind me, I was starting to look like a tramp. Roni had whatever she needed in her carrier bag. Even though she was dressed like a washerwoman she still somehow looked good. That was Roni, she just always carried herself well no matter how much shit she was in. And then I saw the car!

'You are fucking kidding me, Roni. There is no way we

are going to make it to Liverpool in that thing.'

'Well Mister smart arse, we could have taken that big fancy dream car you told me about, but you fucking wrecked it. Get in and stop bloody moaning.' I tried to open the door of the rusty old Citroen 2CV but it would not budge.

'That door does not work, it fell off and I had to jam it back on. You will need to climb over the driver's seat to get in.' Roni said all this without the hint of a smile.

The car was an absolute wreck. I remembered reading that the Citroen 2CV was nicknamed the tin snail. You will have seen them, an iconic car. It was usually featured in those awful arty French films of the sixties. Within minutes we were chugging down the dirt track towards the road. I could feel the wind coming through various openings in the bodywork and my shoes were getting wet as rain dripped down the insides of the windows. 'Roni, as soon as we get to civilisation, we are going to hire a decent fucking car, trust me.'

'Do what you like, you bloody snob. Christ, Matt, you really did turn into a middle-aged bore.' We both laughed, the first time I had laughed properly in years, maybe it was more to do with being hysterical as I surveyed the mess I was in. It was just dawning on me that I did not have my driving license with me or any other documentation. It looked like Bonnie and Clyde would be going all the way to Liverpool in a French rust bucket. I started to dial Charles Cameron Ilderton on my phone.

Charlie was concentrating on trying to focus his camera while at the same time wiping the condensation off the window of the Mondeo. He jumped when the phone buzzed and then cursed as the surprise meant he missed the opportunity to photograph the embracing couple leaving the café.

'Charlie it's me. Don't start fucking talking until I tell you what I need you to do.' I was wasting my breath as usual because P.I. Ilderton ignored me and started babbling with excitement.

'Matt, don't worry the Merc is sorted out. You might need to go and make a statement at the local police station, but it looks ok. Well, maybe not ok as unfortunately, the garage up there reckons the car is a right off. Totally fucked was the words they used, although they did say it had once been a lovely car. A top of the range model, now a pile of scrap. Boy, you do things in style, Mr. Cunningham.'

'Charlie, Charlie, I don't fucking care about the car, listen you need….'

'Listen to this, Matt, just listen to this one. I followed your wife Cara and I might have something.' This made me sit up and listen to him for once.

'Ok Charlie, go on, what is it. Her and the Pilates prick Scott? I knew it.'

'No, no Matt. It was not him, not him at all. You could have bowled me over with a ten-ton truck full of potatoes I was so surprised. Believe it or not and this is hard to believe, trust me. I have just this minute seen her coming out of a café in Fenwick with your friend Eric Carter. Yes, your supposed friend. The guy who put you onto me, I did some work for him with his recent divorce.' I tried not to laugh and ruin his excitement before replying.

'Charlie, don't be so fucking daft. She has probably asked to meet Eric as she will be trying to find out why I have not made any contact.'

'Yes, but mmm, there is more Matt, there is more. If that was all then maybe I would have thought the same thing. The same thing as you Matt, yes the same thing as you.' He was doing that act again where he ekes out every word, every fucking letter as though he has found the secret of eternal youth or the location of the Holy Grail.

'They were kissing Matt, kissing and holding each

other. I swear to God, they were wrapped around each other like a pair of contortionists.'

'Christ, are you sure Charlie. I mean Eric is my best mate, not him surely?' He had hit a nerve and though it sounded unbelievable it kind of fitted with every other crazy thing that had happened to me in the last few weeks.

'I am sure Matt, very sure. I could not be surer if they told me I had won the lottery and I was holding the fucking cheque in my hand.'

Charlie knew he was being economical with the truth, but he had even convinced himself that he had seen what he was describing. In an odd way, he just wanted to please Matt, show him he was getting the information he wanted even if it was grossly exaggerated. Charles Cameron Ilderton needed to feel like a real Private Investigator, not just someone who sat all day in his car waiting to take a picture for endless divorce cases. He needed to be appreciated. He wanted love and attention just like a child. That was because he was a big child, someone who had never grown up. Oh, and as I have already mentioned, Charlie hoped to skin as much money as possible out of this whole affair.

'Ok, Ok Charlie. Good work. Look, I want you to drop all that. I have found Roni and we are driving to Liverpool.

Don't ask me why but there are two things I need you to do. Firstly, meet me in Glasgow, I need you to hire a car for me. Secondly, I am going to text you some details regarding a shopkeeper who was supposedly murdered in Liverpool in the seventies. I want you to dig as deep as you can, find out anything available on it. See what you can come up with. It will take us at least until seven this evening to get to Glasgow. Can you get going on that Charlie?'

'Yes, I will, Matt, of course. I am sorry about the Eric and Cara…' Charlie realised the caller had hung up and he was talking to himself. He sat in his old car and pondered the latest development. This was getting weird now. He was trying to work out what the link might be, Matt Cunningham, Roni Paterson, a supposedly murdered shopkeeper. Maybe this really was going to be his road to riches. The price for his services had just gone up.

Roni looked at me as I finished the call with Charlie boy. I turned and stared at her. Neither of us had ever checked anything about what had happened that day. We had hidden it in a dark corner of our history, never to be spoken about again. Now we had to find out the truth. Did he really die that day and was it treated as a murder at the time? Only the real facts would help us escape the clutches of the elusive V.

I had drifted off and was having one of those car dreams. You know the kind I mean, the one where the noise of the engine and the road stop you from really falling asleep. So, you drift into that no man's land of confusion and abstract reality. This time it was a prison and I was being given a briefing on how to survive my time in jail. *Don't stand out in the crowd, be ready to handle yourself if challenged. Don't curry favour with the guards, the other prisoners will not like it. If you are singled out and attacked then stand your ground and fight back, the other prisoners will respect you. Don't boast about your crime, get to know who is a danger and keep your head down.* The sharp turning of the car woke me. I was soaking in a cold sweat. I would never survive in prison, I knew that for sure. Even thinking about it gave me the fear.

'Roni, you said you spent time in prison. What was it like?' She turned to me with a less than reassuring smile.

'Let's just say that you would not last a day Matt and leave it at that.'

We pulled into a service station just outside Inverness. The little white Citroen had rattled its way through the last 100 miles without completely disintegrating. I felt bad falling asleep and leaving Roni to do the driving. She leaned into the back of the car and opened her plastic bag before pulling out an old purse filled with loose change.

'Jesus Roni, what are you going to do with that? I have my credit cards with me, I will pay for everything. Just so long as you are ok driving to Glasgow and then when we get a hire car I will take over. If I was insured for this heap, I would take a turn.' Roni stopped what she was doing before having a laughing fit.

'Matt, you really are the limit. You are not at a fucking board meeting, this is me, Roni. The car is neither insured, taxed, Mot, fucking anything. You name it, it's not got it. I have not even passed my fucking driving test. Now, are you buying me a coffee or not?' With that, she opened the one usable door and I climbed over the seat to join her. We strolled into the service area and sat at a table. Roni disappeared into the toilet while I went up to order us some food. I was starving, it was dawning on me that I had eaten virtually nothing for days. The adrenalin of V, Roni, Ilderton, and crashing cars had been enough sustenance to keep me moving.

'Matt, Matt Cunningham, is it really you?' I turned to find a middle-aged man and his wife standing in the queue behind me. *Oh, for fuck sake, it was the Macintyre's.*

They lived in the house just four doors down from me and Cara in Whitecraigs. He was some sort of bigwig in the Scottish Government and she played tennis. That was all I knew of them other than to say hello now and then. Cara would moan about us needing to get friendlier with our neighbours, but Gavin Macintyre was just not my kind. He was always bumping on about his golf club and the endless holiday properties he and his wife owned. I turned around and could see the look of shock on his face. Rosemary Glendon Macintyre even took a step back in horror at the apparition in front of her. I will admit I looked a state. My trousers were stained with mud and my shoes had sort of disintegrated. Even though I had washed my face I was still covered in scratches and bruises. For some reason I also had a black eye, it must have been Roni's plant pot.

'Ahh hello Gavin, hello Rosemary. I take it you are heading home after staying at your holiday house in Golspie? I must apologise for the state I am in. I had a wee breakdown in the car this morning and my phone had run out of charge. I Walked across some fields and ended up falling over. A bit of a nightmare to be honest, but all sorted now.' I was desperate to escape but the interrogation was ready to kick in.

'Oh dear, well I hope your lovely wife Cara is not with you. I really cannot imagine her walking across a field in her high heels.' It was a noble attempt by Rosemary to inject some humour into what was a rather awkward situation. I had to think on my feet and the best I could come up with was,

'No, I came up here for a business meeting in Inverness. I am just waiting for a car to pick me up. I can get cleaned up, new suit on and Bob's your uncle.' I could see that neither Gavin nor the esteemed Rosemary Glendon Macintyre was completely convinced with my explanation. To be fair I did look like I had just stepped out of the back of a bin lorry. They might have bought my story if Roni had not chosen to reappear at that point. A gliding vision of flowery dresses, Wellington boots and, beads.

'Fuck me, Matt, the bloody toilets are mobbed, I had to wait in a queue just to get a pee. Have you got the coffee yet? Fucking hell, what have you been doing for the last ten minutes?' I grabbed Roni by the arm and pulled her towards the exit.

'Catch you later Gavin, nice to see you, Rosemary. This is my secretary Angel Benton, she has just arrived to pick me up for the business meeting.' Don't ask me why or how I came up with Angel Benton. It was the first thing that came into my head, I was in a panic and somehow the name seemed to fit the swearing apparition that had just made such a grand entrance. We beat a hasty retreat and purchased sandwiches and coffee from the garage while filling the moving rust bucket up with petrol.

We approached Stirling using B roads. I was desperate to get rid of the Tin Snail now that I knew Roni was an illegal driver. It had been hard work to convince her to stay off the motorway and main roads in case we got pulled by the traffic cops. I suppose she had got away with driving in Kinlochbervie as it was so isolated. The closer we got to the suburbs of Glasgow, the more nervous I became. The Citroen stuck out like a sore thumb. I could see people in other cars pointing and laughing as they overtook us. Roni was, as usual, oblivious to it all, she simply did not care. Rules had been made for others, Roni operated in her own solar system. Trust me, it was a billion light years away from what I and you are used to. I still had the fucking bruises on my head from the plant pot to prove it.

We had agreed to meet Ilderton in the car park at Hamilton Services near Glasgow at 7pm to switch cars. This meant we could avoid most of the city and with a bit of luck the traffic police as well. But you will no doubt guess what was coming next. My luck had been out ever since I first heard the name V and it was not about to change. The rust bucket no longer owned a rear-view mirror and for some reason, I felt compelled to turn around and look behind us. Yes, right on fucking cue, there it was. About half a mile behind, a fast-moving police car lit up with blue lights like some interstellar Christmas tree.

'It is the fucking Police Roni. Jesus, we have had it. I still have the bloody gun in my suitcase. Oh, for fuck sake, this is it, I am going to prison. Oh god help me, why did I get into this mess, what the fuck is going on in my life?'

'Christ Matt, get a grip. You really have turned into the biggest wimp on planet earth.' She had hardly said the words before she did a crazy last-second exit off the main road and onto what looked like a farm track. Even though the tin snail could not go more than 40mph downhill, I still expected to die. And you know what? The bloody Police car carried on flying up the main road, it was nothing to do with us. We did not get away with Roni's Formula one manoeuvre though. Within seconds the Citroen started lurching up and down at the front, it made a horrible clanking sound and then stopped dead. Only the driver's seat belt was working so I was propelled forward and belted my head on the windscreen.

'Oh Jesus, are you ok Matt? I think the car might be fucked. Let me look at your head.' She tenderly rubbed her hands over my brow. We could have been the same two teenagers we had been in the late seventies. I looked at her, for some reason I wanted to laugh. Why did I feel so alive? I was scared stiff about what was happening and what was to come and yet. Maybe it was adrenalin, maybe it was hysteria. I leaned forward, and we kissed, not a wet passionate kiss, just a meeting of our lips for a few seconds.

'I am ok Roni. In fact, I am getting used to being battered about my face, the plant pot was worse.'

The little car was done for. It looked like the front axle had broken as the driving wheels lay at a strange angle. Luckily the track we had ended up on seemed to be unused. Momentum had carried us far enough away from the main carriageway to keep the Citroen hidden.

'I have hardly any charge left in my phone. Let's see where the track takes us too and I will call Charlie, get him to come up here and collect us. We need to find a spot where we can shelter until he can find this place.' I collected my suitcase out of the car and started walking up the little road before bending down to try and fix one of my shoes. The sole was coming away and mud was seeping through the gap and into my toes. It slowly dawned on me that I was talking to myself, Roni was still fussing around the car a few hundred yards away.

'Roni, what are you doing? We are wasting time, come on, get a move on.' The words had hardly left my mouth when a flash of light erupted from the rear of the motor. The crazy bitch had been emptying a can of petrol over the Tin Snail and it was well and truly alight. She was running and so was I.

'In the name of Christ Roni, what the hell was that for?' There was a sudden explosion as our little friend went up in a fireball.

'Never leave any evidence of your past misdeeds Matt. You will learn all this when you do your stretch in prison.' We were both laughing and panting for breath at the same time as we charged up the track.

'Roni Paterson, you are a fucking madwoman.' But I said it with genuine affection.

We eventually came to a row of tumbled down cottages on the edge of a quarry. I need not have worried about Roni attracting attention by setting the car alight. The whole area was covered with burnt out wrecks. Bin bags and household refuse lay strewn amongst the hedges and trees. It seemed that the area was being used as an unofficial dump for those who could not be bothered to book into a council site. No doubt many of the cars had been stolen and used for joy rides before being torched. The rain had started to fall as we sought shelter in the least ruined cottage. I used the last remnants of my phone battery to find our location and call Charlie Boy. He took it all in his stride, I think he was getting used to all this madness in the same way that I was. We found a room at the rear of the building that still had a floor and some semblance of a roof and huddled into the corner to keep warm. It would take Ilderton at least an hour to find this backwater but somehow, I felt good. This was a little oasis of calm and peace from everything that had happened. We still had 24 hours to get to Liverpool, maybe even time to book into a hotel and a shower, eat something, be normal.

I sat there on the damp litter-strewn floor and thought about Cara. *No, surely not. Her and Eric, that cannot be right?* But everything else in my life was so screwed up that even the unthinkable was maybe possible. Roni put her arm around my waist and pulled the two of us closer to get some warmth. Why did it feel so natural for us to be back together, as though the last 35 years had not happened? We said nothing, just sitting there huddled together was enough. Her face was just inches from mine, how could we not end up kissing again?

(Excerpt from official Blackbaron Technologies brochure, 2010)

Matt Cunningham (UK Managing Director) - Matt has been with Blackbaron for almost 26 years. In fact, he originally started with us when we were known as Francis Gernon Manufacturing. Our UK leaders first position was as a line manager. He then had various posts including Software Project Management, HR Operations Management as well as a spell in Sweden working as the lead account manager for one of our biggest customers. It would have surprised few to see Matt eventually get the top UK position.

Liked and respected as a solid pillar of the company, Matt is known to be a people person. Helpful and supportive but also ready to take the lead in re-shaping the future for Blackbaron Technologies. In his spare time, Matt likes to chill out with a good book or a round of golf.

I don't tend to do much in my free time. The company and my work mean everything to me, so when I get home, I like to spend the rest of the day with my family. I suppose you could say I am a normal middle-aged man who just relaxes and enjoys life.

Matt believes that Blackbaron will have some tough decisions to make over the next few years to be able to meet the increased cost pressures of running a modern business.

Sometimes you must make unpopular decisions regarding space allocation and workforce numbers. Blackbaron is one big family and people matter to us. I know each of our employees will give everything to drive the company on to shared success. We support each other and will continue to make sure that anyone we let go is given every help to find suitable future employment.

Let us leave the last word to Matts long-time work colleague and friend Tom Shepherd.

Matt is a fantastic leader. He still wears a suit and tie to work every day. You could maybe say he is old fashioned, but I genuinely feel the way he dresses reflects his personality. He keeps to the middle ground and will never stray off the rails. That is exactly what you want in a leader. Someone who tells the truth and does not believe in keeping things hidden from everyone. His biggest strength is that he is so open and honest. What you see is what you get with Matt.

CHAPTER SIX:
ANGEL BENTON
WELLINGTON BOOTS

(2000)

Roni first set eyes on Giulio in a crowded Milan bar. The new millennium had not long arrived, and the world still had a feeling of innocence, soon to be crushed as the twin towers came down. She was approaching her late thirties and despite the on-off heavy drinking Roni still held onto her figure and good looks. Maybe the fact that she had ceased smoking in her early twenties helped to keep her relatively fresh-faced. And, being an alcoholic does have one advantage. Most heavy drinkers stay slim for the simple reason that eating gets it the way of having a good drink. Maybe the next diet craze sensation will be the two bottles a day diet. Day one, drink a litre of Vodka then sleep until the following morning. Day two, drink two litres of vodka and wake up a week on Wednesday. Guaranteed to make you lose 10 stone in one month.

It did not take long for the blonde alcoholic from Kilmarnock and the dark alcoholic from Cosenza to be sitting side by side. Sipping their drinks while trying to measure each other up. Roni had been in Italy for the last 8 years, jumping between various jobs, looking after children and working in restaurants. Anything to keep her head above water, but gradually her drinking problem meant fewer opportunities until work had virtually dried up. It was not that she did not do a great job, most of her employers loved her wry sense of humour and charm. But no matter how hard she worked, reliability would eventually become the problem. Too much drink the night before or even in the morning would mean no Roni at work that day. She had already asked her mum if she could borrow the air-fare home, that was how close she had come to escaping. They say that opposites attract, not this time. Roni and Giulio were like peas in a pod and the fuse had been lit. Two people with the same irrational emotions and troubled past. Add alcohol into the poisonous mixture and take cover boys and girls, an explosion is coming.

They drank, fought, loved and drank some more for the next two years. Eventually, the days merged into a blur of confused violence and living oblivion. The two became well known in Giulio's home town of Campana nestling in the Southern Italian hills. Roni's mother paid the air-fare, but she did not see her daughter again until the trial.

One morning Roni woke to find herself lying on the kitchen floor. This was not an unusual experience, in fact, she had woken in various places including the bathroom, the garden, even halfway through the front door of the old farm. She would have a burning thirst and a head that ached. It could only be placated by the first drink of the day and that was where she was heading when she crashed over the body of Giulio. A large carving knife lay on the opposite side of the kitchen. Blood was spattered everywhere, on the floor, the walls, even the ceiling. Roni simply picked herself up and continued the journey to the cupboard to drain the last remnants out of every bottle she could find.

Eleven years seemed like a stiff sentence to most. Many gave evidence and the overriding theme pointed the finger at Giulio being a violent man. He had the previous history having assaulted the wife of his two children many times before they separated. He had also been in prison for petty theft and various other drink related crimes. Witnesses painted a picture of a couple who would constantly fight and bicker but would also rely on each other because of alcohol. Some said they had seen or heard Roni giving as good as she got. They make them tough in Kilmarnock. No one really knew what had happened that night. Roni herself when arrested had been found to have stab wounds and many bruises including two black eyes. Whatever the reason, it had been a titanic battle and Roni had imposed a knock out win in the last round.

Her mother wept as she was taken down to start her sentence. But she survived as Roni always did. Her fellow inmates respected the petite Scottish woman for her humour, kind nature, oh and her ability to stand up for herself despite being small and slim. I told you they come out hard in Kilmarnock, were you listening?

(2014)

It was three hours later as dusk descended when we finally saw the headlights of Ilderton's car manoeuvring its way down the track to the dilapidated buildings. By then the cold had started to bite into any part of our bodies not covered by clothing. Being huddled so close to Roni, I could pick up the aroma of incense and scented candles. Unlike Cara, she did not use expensive perfumes, but she still had a sweet fragrance that matched her demeanour despite the Wellingtons. I was annoyed with Charlie boy for taking so long to find us. He told me someone had called his landline just as he was leaving, and he had been forced to chat. With anyone else that statement would have sounded like a lie, not with him. I already knew that Charles Cameron Ilderton would win a gold medal for stretching out even the most meaningless conversation for hours. Roni seemed to like him immediately, I knew it was because both were marginal people. The sort of unconventional characters who live on the edge of normality. Whatever fucking normality means, I had lost sight of it over the horizon. He did have some class though. He had hired a black Jaguar XE. On my money of course.

The decision had been made. Charlie was coming to Liverpool with us. He had not been able to insure the hire car for anyone but himself without documentation and I could no longer take the stress of illegal driving. Something told me that having an extra hired hand on our side might give us an advantage.

'Did you find out anything about the shopkeeper Charlie, the one I asked you to check out?'

'No, nothing yet Matt. I have a contact, an ex-policeman. I give him a bung every now and then and he gets information for me. Fuck knows how he gets it, but he does.'

'Are you sure he is discreet, I mean, can he be trusted?' Ilderton looked at me before replying. I had a feeling he had worked out what my story was. Not that I cared, Charles Cameron Ilderton operated in a mode called cash only. His silence, as well as his loyalty, could be bought.

'Don't worry Matt, he is a bit of a crook anyway. So, he has just as much to lose as you.' The last comment came across as a bit of a threat but Ilderton was playing a dangerous game if he thought he could screw me.

'Well we all have our little secrets don't we Charlie? I still have the gun you got for me.' I left it at that. I would quiz him in private later about Cara and Eric. I still found that one hard to believe but what did it matter now? Everything else was a mess, why not add that one to the equation?

We decided to book into a motel in the remote border village of Abington. It sat nestled in the snow-covered hills halfway between Glasgow and Carlisle. Get cleaned up and leave early, hopefully, be in Liverpool by midday. I had already called my accountant Robin Threshfield before we had left Bendrennon and asked him to meet me. I could tell he did not believe my story about needing cash to buy a boat, but I did not care. I don't think he cared either, he was another one who was easily bought off. Show me an accountant who does not like money, and I will point you in the direction of a hunter who does not enjoy killing. I sat in the back of the Jaguar while Roni chatted to Ilderton up front.

'Charlie, can I ask you a personal question.' I could sense something abstract was coming because Roni did not do normal.

'Sure gorgeous, what is it?'

'Are you married, I mean how could a handsome man like you not have a Mrs. Charlie waiting at home for him?' I wanted to laugh because the large man in the shabby suit driving the car was, well let us just say he was no picture postcard. I decided to settle back and enjoy the entertainment.

'I was married darling but, well she left me. For some reason, she said I drank too much. I don't know why as I hardly touch the stuff. Don't get me wrong, I like the occasional tipple. I mean I would only go to the pub on a Friday, a Saturday and a Sunday, the rest of the week I would just drink in the house. Not every day, I would take a Tuesday off unless it was raining…or sunny. He gave a hearty laugh at his own joke. I suppose that was why I liked him, he could laugh at himself, unlike me.

'Oh, that's a shame, Charlie. Was it definitely because of your drinking, I mean surely, she had a more serious reason to leave you than that?

'What do you mean gorgeous? I was maybe not the best husband in the world, but I never had any affairs. Well not any that she found out about that is.' He snorted with laughter once more at his own joke. At this point, I was thinking Charlie should be on the stage, but maybe one with a guillotine standing on it.

'Oh, I was thinking maybe she left you because….' Roni made a pretence that she was concerned for his feelings and did not want to continue.

'Go on love, tell me what my problem was, I don't mind. She was not my kind anyway.'

'Well, I wondered if she left you because of that god-awful suit you wear?' Both I and Ilderton burst out laughing. Roni simply continued to act as though what she had said was perfectly normal. She was fucking nuts, I knew that for sure. My head still bore the scars. But from that moment our friendly big private investigator became known as The

Suit. It dawned on me that Roni had a habit of giving people nicknames. Why did that make me think back to our teenage days and the original Liverpool trip?

Rosemary Glendon Macintyre walked with a purpose towards the big electric gates of the Cunningham home. Ever since arriving back at their own large house in Glenrodding Avenue the previous evening, she had been desperate to speak to Cara. Break the bad news before that strange husband of hers Matt arrived back from his supposed business trip. Gavin had been against her mentioning the encounter at the service station. He could sympathise with Matt, he understood his neighbour had been caught out. But Gavin could never stop Rosemary Glendon Macintyre from doing anything she wanted. She was a woman on a mission, and she was looking forward to digging the hole that she wanted to see Matt fall into.

Cara poured the expensive coffee into the two mugs and handed one to Rosemary. The two women had never really been over friendly, the occasional chat about the weather in passing but that was about it. Cara knew that the woman sitting on the kitchen stool opposite her was at that dangerous age where she was losing the ability to be sensitive to other's feelings. She was like one of those ancient aunties you had when you were first married. *Ooh, I see you have been enjoying a few cakes, Jim.* What she really meant was, *Jim, you are a fat bastard.* In fact, give her another few years and she would probably say those exact words.

Cara had her defences up already. Whatever old Rosemary Glendon Macintyre was about to hit her with, she was going to keep a stiff upper lip. Damage limitation was all she could do as she waited for the opening salvo.

'I thought it best to come and see you, Cara. We met your husband Matt at the service area near Stirling on the way back from one of our other homes in Golspie.' Even the words, *your husband* sent warning signals. It was like an accusation, as though Cara had done something wrong by being married to Matt.

'Oh yes, he is away on a week-long hiking trip in the Highlands. He must have been driving to a different mountain range.' As soon as the words were out Cara knew she had blown it. She inwardly cursed herself for jumping in with a reply before letting Rosemary tell the whole story'

'Oh, that is odd because he told us he was on a business trip. His personal assistant was with him. I think he said she was called Angel Benton or something like that.' Cara tried desperately to think on her feet. She had lost the battle but maybe she could retreat without complete surrender.

'Oh, Oh yes. I know Angel quite well. Knowing Matt, he will be mixing work with pleasure. Miss. Benton will be meeting him for a few hours, probably getting documents signed or something.' Cara could feel her face going red. The hole she was digging had just got deeper.

'Oh, mixing business with pleasure, I see.' Rosemary rolled her eyes as she said the words with a tone of heavy sarcasm. Well, it was rather odd Cara, rather odd.' Cara sighed, she wanted to raise a white flag and start waving it. Admit defeat and surrender before the old lady twisted the knife in.

'Rather odd, in what way Rosemary?'

'Well, his supposed personal assistant was wearing Wellington boots. She looked like one of those hippy farmers and her language was quite frightful. I mean, she used that word.'

'And what word was that Rosemary?'

'She used that dreadful F word and not just once. I mean, her a business lady as well. Oh, and Matt was covered in mud, come to think of it, so was his friend, I mean personal assistant, Miss Benton!'

I stepped out of the shower in my room at the motel,

it felt good to be clean again. I had shocked myself when I looked in the mirror, bruises, yellow marks around my eyes and in desperate need of a shave. We had taken three separate rooms and agreed to meet in the restaurant of the hotel in an hour. It was one of those travel motels attached to a motorway service area in the middle of nowhere. The Suit had complained it did not even have a pub nearby but considering I was with one possible alcoholic and one definite recovering alcoholic, maybe that was a good thing. I just wanted to get to Liverpool and do whatever V wanted, pay the going price and forget this whole damn thing. If I could have found out who my tormentor was, I would have kicked their teeth in or maybe even used the gun. It was not the fact they were demanding money and a free ride, it was because they were tormenting me. I would have liked to think it was both of us that was suffering but somehow Roni seemed to be on another plane. One that existed simply for her while everything else floated around with little or no substance.

There was a knock at the door. I quickly threw on my clothes and opened it to allow Robin Threshfield, my accountant to enter. 'Hi Matt, how are you?'

'I am good Robin. Look I am sorry for putting you in

this position but the opportunity to buy the boat is a one-off. They want cash and I don't want to miss out.' I could tell he was looking at the marks on my face and wondering what the hell was going on.

'It is ok Matt, don't worry about it.' He placed the black case on the bed.

'Did you manage to get it all Robin?'

'Every penny Matt, 250,000 pounds in cash.' We dispensed with the niceties as I wanted him gone as quickly as possible. Neither of us wished to talk too much in case the truth came out. He accepted the charade about needing money to buy a boat. No, let's be honest and re-phrase that. He accepted my story because I had just made him 50k richer. As I mentioned before, accountants love money, especially when it ends up in their pockets. Within ten minutes of knocking the door, he was on the road back to Glasgow.

The time I had been dreading had arrived. Before leaving my room, I knew I had to call Cara, let her know everything was fine and that I was happily tramping the hills of Scotland while enjoying my enforced solitude. You probably already know that the conversation did not turn out the way I expected it to. How on earth did I keep getting surprised at being surprised? My world had turned upside down since that first note arrived. Why would the next step and the next and the next not turn out to be just as absurd? She picked up my call within seconds, maybe even less than seconds.

'Hi Cara, its…'

'Who the fuck is Angel Benton?' I knew this was serious because Cara rarely lost her temper and to swear was unheard of.

'Who, oh Angel. She is a work colleague, I met her at the Stirling Services, she…'

'Don't lie to me, Matt. She was with you, who the hell is she? Matt, what the fucking hell is going on?'

'Look, Cara, I will explain everything in time. Just give me two more days and you will understand. I need you to stay calm and trust me, can you do that?'

'Stay fucking calm?' She was becoming hysterical now as she became angrier. 'I just had that old cow Rosemary around. Who the hell is Angel Benton and why was she wearing fucking Wellington boots?'

I wished I had not lost my temper, maybe all the emotion of the past six days just took over.

'You ask me what is going on. What the fuck are you

doing kissing Eric? Or is it Scott or fucking every guy you meet.'

After that, it descended into a slanging match with Cara accusing me of being both jealous and insane. I cut her off and put her calls on mute again. There was no point in trying to explain my situation, how could I? It would only be sorted out once and for all when I paid off the mysterious V and went back home.

In the room next door, The Suit sat reading the email on his phone. To his credit, he had managed to build up a list of associates over the years who could supply answers to his questions. He liked to refer to them as his contacts, it made everything sound more sinister than it really was. Carter Jolley, no I am serious, that was his name, was an ex-Police detective. He liked The Suit, most people did. That was because most of Charlie's contacts tended to be like him. Dreamers and drinkers who lived in a world of both fantasy and reality. Carter Jolley had been forced to resign from the Police force some years ago due to his habit of making up incidents that simply did not happen. He would pride himself to his colleagues with tales of how proper policing did not always mean an arrest. *A warning from me was all it needed rather than go in heavy handed.* Of course, the people and the warnings did not exist but The Rose and Crown for a few pints did.

The Suit sighed and stood up to stretch his arms. The content in the email was not what he had wanted to read. It did not help him in his quest to milk as much money out of Matt Cunningham as possible. But as I already mentioned, The Suit lived in a world where it was easy to blur the lines between fact and fiction. He picked up his crushed jacket and headed off to the restaurant to tell Matt what he wanted him to hear.

I walked across the car park from the motel to the service area. A mix of fast food outlets and shops selling overpriced sweets, magazines and the sort of clothes only a tramp would wear. The car park was thinning out as the motorway quietened down. It was after 10pm and a dark wet mist was settling in around the fluorescent-lit complex. The Suit was sitting alone in the restaurant with a smile beaming across his face. I could instantly see why.

'Where did you get the beer from Charlie?'

'Well Matt, that is, in my opinion, a very good question and one that deserves a well-tuned answer.' *Oh, for fuck sake*, I thought to myself.

'The restaurant is licenced, Matt. They sell alcohol so

long as you are an overnight guest at the motel. We can even take it back to our rooms, have a wee party. Shall I get you one?'

'No thanks, Charlie. Look, I need to speak to you. Get things sorted out before Roni joins us.'

'Yes, yes of course Matt. But let me tell you first. I have news back from my contact in the force. A chap who goes by the name of Carter, Carter Jolley. He was a major player in the Police, retired with honour. Well respected by the top brass. A man who was known for good old-fashioned Policing.' I grasped his arm with my hand.

'Will you please get to the fucking point, Charlie.' He knew I meant business.

'Birkby, the Liverpool shopkeeper. The one you asked me to check out.' I sat up now and listened. Every nerve froze as my whole body waited. Even in the few seconds, it took The Suit to deliver the punchline I prayed that he would tell me Birkby had survived and the incident had been long forgotten. We could all leave that night and go back to our own homes. Ok, one of us would have to give Roni a lift back up North. Maybe I could pay for a taxi? You must be asking yourself, why does this guy keep hoping something positive will happen when we both know damn well what is coming?

'It is not good news Matt.' I sat back in resignation.

'My contact, he is an ex-policeman, did I tell you that? Name of Carter Jolley. A nice chap.' I no longer cared. I let The Suit ramble on until some minutes later he finally got to the words that mattered.

'So, it seems that Birkby was murdered but the case was never solved. A witness supposedly saw two local youths running from the shop but despite trawling through every Liverpudlian scallywag, they could not get any solid leads. I suppose unless someone comes forward with new information, then the case will forever remain a mystery.' Charlie emphasised the *unless someone comes forward* part. The time had come for us to strike a deal, we both knew it.

I told Charlie everything, to the last detail. I asked him not to tell Roni that it was confirmed as murder. She was unstable enough, I felt it best to wait until we got to Liverpool and V contacted us. I suppose the final price I agreed with The Suit was both payment for his services as well as blackmail money. We both knew he could not grass me up and that he had to help me pay off V. That was the only way he would walk away with the money he wanted. The contract was signed as I transferred 100k into his account using my laptop. The other 100k would follow once the job was done and we went our separate ways. There was no way out of this for The Suit now, he had accepted the payment. Charlie boy was now covering up for a murderer and if V exposed me then he was coming down as well.

The Suit went up to the little bar that was separated from the rest of the restaurant. I suppose he was celebrating the deal. I would have had a drink to drown my sorrows, but I knew tomorrow would be the day. I had to keep my wits intact, I sensed that V might not be paid off as easily as The Suit had been.

'There is some amazing stuff on sale here Matt. Some fucking great gear and nicely priced too.' I jumped in my seat as Roni appeared and dumped herself down opposite me. She had showered, her grey and blonde hair a cascade of unruly curls that flowed around her face. Looking at her made me realise how young she still seemed. It was odd that despite having lived through untold horrors in her time, she still seemed more innocent than me. I was the cosseted one and yet life had made me weary and impatient of everyone and everything.

'Are you serious Roni? The stuff they sell in this place is junk. What the hell have you got in that plastic bag?'

'It might be junk to you Cunningham because you can afford to pay for expensive shit. I might be poor, but I have self-respect. Plus, I know a good bargain when I see one, so fuck you, Mister Rich guy.' I laughed before replying.

'Roni, I will buy you whatever you want. Once we get this blackmail shit out of the way, I will take you shopping in Liverpool. Get you some expensive clothes, a hairdo, whatever you fucking desire.' She leaned over the table towards me before grabbing my hair and pulling my face close to hers.

'Cunningham, I don't want your money. You can stick your wallet up your arse and shove it sideways. I have survived fine by myself for the last 35 years so screw you.' She was still smiling as she said the words, even if she was serious.

'Ok Roni, what is it you have bought that is such a great fucking bargain?' She let go of my hair and sat back before placing her hands inside the plastic bag. A look of triumph written across her face as she pulled the multicoloured flowered Wellington boots out and stood them side by side before me.

'£3.99 a fucking pair. I told you I could spot a bargain, Matt. I only had £4.25 left in my coin bag as well.'

Cara regretted losing her cool so quickly when Matt called. And yet, who could blame her? She had just been told that her husband had been seen in Stirling with some strange woman called Angel Benton who wore Wellington boots. She knew he would put his phone back on mute after the row and that the opportunity to find out what the hell was going on had gone. Cara sat in the kitchen nursing her coffee while trying to make sense of it all. Maybe she had always had a feeling that something strange was happening. It would have been easier if it was an affair, but the whole scenario did not fit together. If it was simply another woman then why disappear? The two of them lived virtually separate lives, he could have easily hidden it from her. No, it was worse than that, it had to be. Cara could sense that this could involve them all, and not in a good way. She worried for Matt, but she was even more concerned about the implications for both herself and their daughter.

The mobile phone she had left beside the coffee maker started buzzing and Cara wearily stepped off the kitchen stool to retrieve it. But she had only gone a few steps when instinct made her look down at the kitchen waste paper basket. Mary would usually empty it but with her mother taking another bad turn she had not been back since the day

Matt left. It was almost empty except for Cara's discarded plastic water bottle and a few tomatoes she had dumped from the fridge. It was what lay underneath that caught her attention. Myriad pieces of ripped up white paper that had obviously been a single page written note. Cara carefully unfolded that day's newspaper on top of the breakfast bar and emptied the contents of the bin onto it. She wretched while removing the remains of the tomatoes that had seeped into the little bits of paper.

It could be nothing but whoever had ripped up the note had taken care to make sure that rebuilding it was going to be difficult. Every ten minutes her phone would buzz but Cara was lost in her own world of jigsaw puzzles and strange women wearing Wellington boots. It was incredibly frustrating work.

Mcmhang, the time running pay now.

She still had more than half of the little pieces of tomato stained paper stretched out on the table. It was the opening word that she could not get right. It was familiar but no matter what permutation she attempted it would not work. Cara looked back into the wastepaper basket and then she saw the three missing pieces stuck to the side of the bin. Once the first letters fell into place, it became easier to fill out the rest of the sentence.

Cunningham, the time has come to stop running.

Cara knew by the amount of paper left that one more sentence was coming. She felt dizzy with fear, holding her breath at the horror unfolding. And then it was complete, the sentence staring back at her. 25 years of marriage to a man she thought she knew. The head of the company, the golf and tennis player, the father of her daughter, the man who everyone thought of as middle of the road Matt. 25 years of living a lie and not once had she ever doubted that she was married to a pillar of society.

Cunningham, the time has come to stop running. You are a murderer and now you must pay. V

The Suit returned with another bottle of beer in his hand and sat down beside Roni. The two of them facing me. The new multicoloured Wellington boots acting as a barrier as they sat between us on the table.

'Nice boots Matt, they suit you.' I got the joke, but Roni just acted as though it went over her head.

'They are mine Mr. Suit, do you like them?'

'I know gorgeous, I was just kidding. They are crackers. I bet you paid a fortune for them. Are they designer boots by any chance?' Roni perked up at the compliment. She was proud of her purchase and either did not understand The Suit's irony or just chose to ignore it.

'£3.99.' Roni sat back with a look of innocent pride on her face. It was hard not to admire the woman who could handle prison with ease and yet be so excited by a pair of cheap plastic boots. The Suit was on a roll now. I could tell he fancied Roni and was trying desperately to both impress and make her laugh.

'What £3.99! For each boot? Wow, I love a girl who can spot a bargain.' He gave her a light poke on the arm, and she responded by flicking her finger across the end of his nose.

Oh, for fuck sake, I thought to myself. *And these two are going to help me escape the clutches of the clever and elusive V?* I could not help but laugh though.

Cara was still shaking as she gathered the little scraps of paper together and placed them into a plastic bag. The word *murderer* was crashing around in her head, searching for a place to land and be accepted. But it was impossible, nothing in her memory banks could equate that kind of horror with anything she had experienced before. Friends, family, coffee mornings, the church, Pilates classes, Matt, Simone, dinner parties, marriage, falling out, making up, childbirth, cancer scares, her father passing away, Mary the home help, holidays, sunburn, laughing, crying, smiling, arguing, doubting God, praying to God, television, new cars, making the dinner, going shopping, planting the summer pots, tidying up after her daughter, filling out forms, doing her hair, putting on make-up, getting dressed, sleeping, worrying, staying alive…nowhere for the words to settle down and find a home. Murderer, murderer, murderer… Matt, Matt, Matt.

She looked up from the quicksand that was enveloping every part of her body, dirty filthy mud sliding and squelching as it dragged her further down into the bog. Her phone was buzzing, the same way it had been on and off for the last few hours. Cara climbed out of the black tide that gripped her soul and suddenly felt alive, maybe for the first time in years. It was a mother's instinct, she would die before she would accept defeat. *You bastard Matt, you fucking bastard. Whatever it is you have done, I will not let you destroy me and Simone as well.* She picked up the phone. It was Eric, she knew it would be.

'Cara, it's Eric. I spoke to Charles Cameron Ilderton some hours ago. I have been trying to phone you.'

'I know you have Eric. Did you find anything out?'

'Yes. He would not tell me exactly what was going on but Ilderton loves talking and he did say something.'

'Yes, yes, go on Eric, what was it?'

'Well, Ilderton seems to be fully employed by Matt now. I was lucky because I caught him at his office just before he left to go and pick up your husband just outside Stirling. Charlie is only answering calls from Matt on his mobile so that is why it has been so difficult to get hold of him.'

'Did he say why he needed to go and get him? Matt has his car with him. Why would he need a lift?' There was hesitation at the other end of the line, as though Eric was afraid to tell Cara what he had heard next.

'Eric, just tell me everything. It no longer matters. You will understand when I explain.'

'Ok Cara. Well, you did say you wanted to hear this. According to Ilderton, Matt has wrecked his car and needed him to bring a hire car. But that is not all. For some reason, he says that Matt needs to go to Liverpool, and he has some woman called Roni Paterson with him.' Cara should have been shocked, but the word murderer had the ability to make everything else seem normal.

'Roni Paterson, who the hell is Roni Paterson? What

the hell happened to Angel Benton?

'Cara, I have absolutely no idea who any of these people are. Ilderton said he had to go and would not tell me anymore.' But Cara was no fool. Already her instinct had started to piece together the few facts she had. Maybe not enough to give the whole story but enough for her to be able to put a survival plan in place. There was no way she was going to sit around and fret, this was her marriage, her money and her child that was at stake. The name Roni Paterson was bringing back vague memories of Matt's stories from his younger days. Somehow, she had already worked out that Angel Benton and Roni Paterson might be the same person. Cara had climbed out of the filthy bog now and said the next sentence with a steely determination. It was not a request, it was an order. One that she knew Eric would agree to. How could he not? She knew he was infatuated with her.

'Eric, I think Matt is being blackmailed. I need to go to Liverpool, and I want you to come with me. Don't ask why or what we can do. I just know that is what I need to do.'

The Suit slugged the rest of his beer down and then decided he wanted something a little stronger. Despite my protestations about needing to keep our wits intact for tomorrow, he ignored me and walked off to buy a bottle of wine. I was worried about him drinking in front of Roni if she was an ex-alcoholic. It could also have been me disliking the fact they seem to be getting on so well. Why did I always feel the need to control everything? I was not at work now, employees would do as I requested. I could pay The Suit to follow my orders, up to a point. And Roni? She would do exactly as she wanted. Nothing could buy her.

'I am going to crash out Roni. It is getting late, might be a good idea for both of us to get a good sleep and recharge for whatever is coming our way tomorrow.'

At that point, The Suit returned to the table with the bottle and three glasses.

'Come on guys, share a drink with me. It is hardly going to kill us for fuck sake.' I stood up to make it clear I was going to my bed. I wanted to give Roni the chance to follow me. She turned around to face me and smiled sympathetically, making me feel like a dismissed schoolboy.

'I will see you in the morning, Matt. It is too early for me, I will keep Mr. Suit company if you don't mind.' The Suit looked at me with a smug smile. He had got one over on me and it obviously made him feel good. I suppose he deserved it. I could not help but admire my two companions although I felt left out. I could have stayed and had a drink, but it would mean losing face now. So, I said my goodbyes and walked off back to the motel.

I lay on the bed and tried to piece everything together. Tomorrow would be Friday, five days since I had read the note sent to the house. So much had happened in such a short time. How had I gone from being a few weeks from retirement to this? A lonely motel with two crazy companions. A wrecked car, a crumbling marriage and about to lose a lot of money. V was controlling my every move. Whoever it was had my life in the palm of their hand. What would they ask of me at six pm in Liverpool tomorrow? I tried to close my eyes and get some sleep, but it was impossible. I was worried about Roni, once she started drinking with The Suit anything could happen. I imagined police sirens as the two of them ended up in a drunken fight, either with each other or with the staff. She was a ticking time bomb just waiting to be ignited once again. He was the perfect catalyst and would strike the match that would no doubt cause the explosion. You are probably thinking, *I know what the real problem is Matt.* And you would be right. I was jealous, annoyed that she had discarded me for The Suit. Given up her new-found sobriety so quickly because he made her laugh.

At long last, I started to drift off to sleep. The dreams coming in early, before I had completely left the world of reality. I could still sense the dark room surrounding me even though I was now in a prison cell. The inmates hated me, I knew they were coming to teach me a lesson. Beat the living shit out of the posh well-spoken Glaswegian. I was not one of them, stuck out like the big softie I was. But why would they knock so quietly on the door? The hardened criminals of Liverpool tapping gently as though they were frightened to enter my room. I woke abruptly and sat up. Someone was indeed knocking quietly on the plastic frame. I turned on the light and stumbled over to open the door. Slowly I edged it wide, expecting to see a policeman or the motel manager standing there. It was neither of them. It was Roni and she was stone cold sober. But we know by now that Roni does not do normal even if she had not had a drink. She was completely naked except for the brand new multicoloured Wellington boots attached to the bottom of her legs.

'For Christ sake Matt, let me in, it is bloody freezing out here.' I was still holding the door while trying my best not to laugh. She pushed past me and throwing the boots off she jumped into the bed I had just vacated.

'I thought you had an exciting night planned with your dream man, The Suit.' She laughed and pulled the duvet up, so it covered everything except her face.

'Ooh, do I detect a hint of jealousy Mr. Big Shot Cunningham.'

'What? Me jealous of Charlie and his suit? Give me a break.' I hurried over to the bed and climbed in.

'For fuck sake, Roni, move over will you, it's bloody freezing in here.' We were both laughing now. She put her feet on top of mine at the bottom of the bed.

'Are you glad I came to your room, Matt?'

'Yes and no.' I replied.

'Eh, what the fuck do you mean Cunningham?'

'I mean no because your feet are fucking freezing and yes because I love a lady who can spot a bargain. £3.99 for a pair of Wellington boots Roni. Wow, get you.'

Email from Carter Jolley (Ex Policeman/ Part-time daydreamer) to The Suit (Full-time daydreamer) (2014)

Hello Charlie, Hope things are hanging well with you old boy? Been a while since the two musketeers went on the razzle in Glasgow and had the girls quaking in their shoes. Let's get another night soon. We could get my old police partner Bobbie Nutbussle along, make it The Three Musketeers. The girls love Bobbie, always has a harem following him.

Anyway, I got that information you wanted old chap. It was not that hard to find, so no need for cash, just pay for the beers on our night out. I think the guy you enquired about was a local shopkeeper Reg Birkby. He ran a grocery store on Sefton Street in Liverpool during the seventies and eighties. His son Tommy helped him out. I think the incident you asked about happened in the late summer of 1978. According to the local press at the time, his shop was robbed by two teenagers, one male, and one female. He described them as having Scottish accents. He was quoted at the time as saying he tried to stop them escaping and he tripped over, fell on a broken bottle and was knocked unconscious. The pair left him for dead but lucky for him a local woman Maureen Quine came into the shop a few moments later. She described the two teenagers she saw running away but it was difficult as they had their backs to her. They jumped in a car, but she did not get the registration.

I know you mentioned it might have been a murder case but sorry to disappoint you, Charlie. From what I can gather Reg Birkby survived. He became a bit of a local celebrity as despite being on death's door having lost so much blood, he was back running his shop three months later. He retired in 1987 and his son ran the shop for a few years after. I cannot find anything more about him after that date. The police at the time did try to trace the culprits but the trail went cold after a while. I don't see any likelihood of the investigation being re-opened as Reg the shopkeeper survived and even admitted that the fall had been more of an accident than anything else.

I Hope that is the information you were looking for Charlie. As I mentioned, no need to pay me, although a wee loan of a few hundred quid would not go amiss. They charge almost 4 bloody pounds for a pint at my local these days. You work hard all your life supporting the community, fighting the criminals and what do you get? Kicked out of the force for no good reason. It is all softly softly now, a pat on the back and don't be a naughty boy again. No wonder the country is going to the dogs. I bet the Police don't even drink on duty anymore, it's a bloody disgrace. They pay illegal immigrants to sail over here and live in luxury and us hard working ex-coppers can hardly get a good drink in. Don't get me started.

See you soon old chap. Don't forget the loan.

P.S. Nilaksh said to say hello and if you are ever in Maryhill then pop round and she will make a curry. I don't know how she still puts up with me. I think Indian women are easier going than Scottish ones. Maybe that is why I married her.

CHAPTER SEVEN:
LEATHER FACE
LOVES ROSIE
CHEEKS

(2014)

I lay in the bed unable to sleep and watched the cold Scottish dawn seep through the thin curtains of the motel bedroom. This was it, D-day had arrived. Today all this madness would end one way or another. I had never been so certain of anything in my life. Maybe I did not know what the outcome would be, but something told me it would not end well. Someone was going to be the new victim, they had to be. V, Roni, me and The Suit. Four people, it was almost like I was back in my punk band again. Another toxic mix that could only end in disaster.

Roni lay curled up in a little ball beside me. She looked so frail and tiny, almost like an apparition, a silent warm shadow that had followed me forever from the past. I thought back to the cave in Sammington, the last time the two of us were allowed to be happy in each other's company. Innocent kids on an exciting expedition without a care in the world. Had Birkby not happened maybe both our lives would have been so different? A stupid reflex, sending him sprawling to the floor and our dreams died. Roni finally moved as if to prove she was still alive, her head snuggling into my chest. 'It's a fucking shame, Matt.'

'What is a fucking shame, Roni?

'You could have saved yourself a fortune.'

'What are you talking about Roni? How could I save myself a fortune?' She lifted her face up towards mine.

'We could have saved on a room. You paid for two rooms you idiot, I have hardly used mine.' I laughed although as always with Roni, I was never sure if she was being serious or just taking the mickey.

'Roni, for fuck sake, the room cost £32. Do you know how much I am worth? This day might end with me in fucking jail and you seriously think I give a fuck about an extra £32?' She poked me in the ribs before replying.

'There you go again, talking about how much money you have Cunningham. Do you know that money is the root of all evil?' She bounced out of bed before dragging on the new Wellington boots. And, she was so right. Money was the exact reason I was in this situation.

'Roni, I was laying here thinking back to the cave you took me to see in that little village. Do you remember? It was on the way to Liverpool all those years ago, before things went wrong.' She looked at me for a few seconds before replying.

'Bruce's cave, it was called Matt. It was in Sammington. How strange you should remember. It is a moment I have carried with me all my life. Do you recall what I said when you pulled me back from the edge of the path that day?' And the odd thing was, I did. Vividly.

'I do remember Roni. You said, we could jump together into another world.' We gazed at each other for a while longer. It was then that I realised we should never have parted. She finally broke the spell and turned to leave.

'What are you doing?'

'I am going back to my room to get a shower and get dressed. No point in wasting Mister Rich guy Cunningham's millions now is there?' She winked at me before her naked figure disappeared out of the door.

'Roni, wait, there is something I have not told you.'

'What is it, Matt, for fuck sake, it is freezing. You could

have told me that you still adore me before I got out of that nice warm bed.'

'No, I am being serious Roni. The Suit, I mean Charlie. He found out what happened to him, Birkby, after we ran away.' I hated breaking the closeness we had just shared with the bad news. Roni walked back into the room and sat on the end of the bed.

'Go on then, tell me what The Suit discovered that we don't already know.'

'He died Roni, the shopkeeper died, we know for sure now. It was murder, that is how it was viewed at the time.' I had expected her to be shocked, look sad, maybe even cry. She stared back at me, almost expressionless.

'Well if That is what The Suit says happened, who are we to doubt it Matt.' And then the walking nude in the Wellington boots stood up and left the room.

Cara had no real plan or even a logical reason why she was driving to Liverpool from Glasgow. Since she had salvaged the note from the bin her world had turned on its head. She had to do something, feel as though she could influence the outcome of the impending disaster. Matt would make contact eventually and when he did, she wanted to be close by.

Eric said very little as he sat in the passenger seat watching the M74 snake through the snow-lined border hills. His own emotions were spinning at the sudden change in circumstances. He tried to convince himself that he wanted to help Matt, but Cara was the real reason he was here. She had told him about the blackmail note.

Cunningham, the time has come to stop running. You are a murderer and now you must pay. V

Eric had spent many a drunken night or a golf weekend with his friend. Nothing had ever pointed to this. Matt had mentioned his colourful past as a youth but involved in a murder! The whole thing was crazy, but every cloud has a silver lining. He was in a car with the woman he had feared, admired and lusted after for years. Eric had tried to make some sense of it all to Cara, could it be a hoax? Was the note some elaborate cover for something Matt was involved in? Nothing added up though and Eric remained as confused as Cara. One thing he did know was that another marriage was falling apart and this time it was not his. Once the dust had settled and the mystery solved Eric knew Cara would be a free agent. He must be in with a shout, she had asked him along in her hour of need after all.

A sign, Abington Services 2 miles, flashed passed as

the large Range Rover ate up the road with ease. 'Eric, I need to stop and get petrol, plus I am dying for a coffee. Would you be a darling and nip in and get me one while I try to call Matt again?

'Of course, Cara, no problem.'

She steered the car around the winding road that edged the service area car park and pulled into an empty space. Little white specs of snow floated down to be crushed into a dirty brown slush as cars entered and exited the rest area. Cara turned off the ignition and pushed herself back in the seat. For the first time since reading those words, she felt tired and empty. What on earth was she doing, chasing an illusion? Trying to follow the man she no longer knew, the man she had never really known. Suddenly Cara started to cry, the tears welling up and trickling down her cheeks. She felt completely alone. The woman who was always in control of her emotions was now a little girl lost, isolated in a world of falling snow and emptiness. She felt Eric's hand on her leg, he was trying to comfort her, but Cara understood. He was making the first move to establish his long-term aim. Making a statement that he would help her get through this. And when it was all over, then maybe the two of them?

'I am ok Eric, Sorry. I suppose things have just got

on top of me suddenly. How about you go and get those coffees?' He started to move his hand away from her leg but not before giving what was supposed to be a reassuring squeeze. They both understood it was more than that.

'Two white coffees coming up Cara. I hope you manage to get through to Matt.'

She watched Eric disappear through the doors into the service area. Her phone lay beside her on the leather tray that separated the driver's seat from the one he had just vacated. Cara re-started the car engine and drove out of the car park. Something made her look at the Motel that stood a few hundred yards away from the main service area. She smiled ruefully to herself as she thought about the cheap little rooms that no doubt harboured a million secrets. Clandestine couples escaping their real lives in the hope of re-discovering something that they had never had in the first place. Married men and women trying to convince themselves that life with someone else would solve all their problems.

Cara laughed for the first time since she had pieced the note back together. She laughed at the thought of Eric standing in the snow holding two plastic cups of coffee while he tried to figure out why he could not find the car.

And then she turned the steering wheel to head over the bridge and go back to Glasgow. Why chase something that was over? Matt was finished, they were finished. No matter what happened now she would be a free woman. Shame and humiliation might be heading her way but that was better than trying to save someone she no longer cared about. She pressed the keys on her phone and blocked any calls from Matt. Her daughter was the only thing that mattered now. Matt would be either dead or in prison, either way, Cara did not want to hear from him again.

The Suit was in the driving seat with me beside him. Roni was in the back with her legs stretched out and her head propped up against one of the side windows. We had already passed the last of the three motorway exits for Carlisle. Light snow floated across the road driven by the wind. The Satnav in the Jaguar spoke in a soft female voice to tell us it would take 2 hours and 17 minutes. 'Three hours should get us to Liverpool, that will give us a few hours until that bastard V makes contact at 4.' I felt slightly ridiculous talking about V as a person. We had no idea whether they were man, woman or dog.

'2 hours 17 minutes I think you will find Matt. That is what Glenda said.' I turned around to look at the voice from the back of the car.

'Who the fuck is Glenda?' Roni ignored me and turned her attention to The Suit.

'What time did you get to your bed then last night Mister Suit?'

'It was not long after you left, gorgeous. I took the bottle back to my room, it is not a lot of fun drinking on your own. I knocked on your door to see if you wanted a nightcap, but you must have been asleep or maybe out for a midnight walk.' The Suit nudged me and winked. At least he did not hold any grudges after I had inadvertently stolen Roni from his grasp.

'You should have slept in the car last night for some company.' I could see a Roni type statement was coming.

'Company, what are you on about gorgeous?'

'Glenda, you could have chatted up Glenda the woman in the car who tells us where we are going and when we will get there.' While I listened to this bizarre conversation, I could see Roni messing about with my holdall. There was no point in asking her why she was rifling through my clothes as no matter what I said, she would do it anyway. She finally found what she was looking for, the plastic bag with the gun in it.

'Put your hands in the air you mutha fucka.' Roni had the end of the gun held against the back of The Suits head.

'You have been watching too many films gorgeous. Anyway, you shoot me, and we all die. A bit of advice my dear Roni. Never shoot the driver when he is driving.' The Suit was laughing, enjoying the attention from Roni. I felt nervous, even though she was just messing about, the last thing I needed was someone fucking about with a gun. And if that someone was Roni then even more so.

'Roni, stop pissing around. That gun is real and anyway, all we need is someone in another car to see it and call the police. Put the fucking thing away and act your age.' She placed the gun back inside my suitcase with mock indignation.

'You always have to act the adult don't you big shot Matt. What the fuck did I ever see in you when we were young.' Even though Roni was pretending to mock me, I sensed she was digging for something from The Suit. That was Roni, she would act like a child while underneath the surface she was working things out.

'So, Mister Suit. Matt tells me you sourced the gun from one of your gangland contacts in Glasgow?' I could tell that The Suit was uncomfortable with the question because he took a few seconds to answer. Normally he would grab every opportunity to talk in an attempt to stop anyone else getting a word in.

'Err, yes. One of my contacts. Cost me a small fortune. Guns are not easy to get hold of gorgeous, trust me on that one.' Roni laughed before taking her feet off the seat and sitting up straight.

'Is that so Mister Suit? Well if you say it then it must be true.' I kept silent and for once Ilderton did not reply. Roni was no fool, maybe The Suit had impressed me, but she was far too streetwise to be taken in by a low-grade conman and she was letting him know.

(2013)

He was a very large man. Not someone you would just walk past and maybe think, *wow he is a big guy.* No, he was one of those people you would try not to look at but once he was out of earshot you would nudge your partner and say, *did you see the fucking size of that guy?* Now look, before you start, I am not fat shaming anymore than I would thin shame, someone. Surely if you look at a person and think, that guy looks after himself then that is no better or worse than saying, check him, who ate all the chocolate bars? So,

I am not being fattest, thinnest or anything-ist. I am simply describing this new character in my tale and making the point that he was big, fucking enormous in fact.

The sweat was running down his brow even though he lay on the bed and hardly moved. He knew the final warning had been issued. It was not as though he had deliberately set out on a plan to be unhealthy and overweight. It just happened gradually, too much food and too much drinking. As each year passed the problem increased. At times, he had tried to cut back, even go on a diet and be alcohol-free, but the same pattern would creep back in. But this was it, the ultimatum had arrived as he knew it eventually had to. He might recover from a heart attack, but the possibility of a leg amputation meant no going back. He swore on his mother's grave that he would start the slow process that might save his life and at that point he really meant it.

The nurse came into the room to give him his medication. She pulled the curtains of the window wider. The sun was shining over the green fields outside. The large new hospital on the outskirts of Kilmarnock at least offered a sylvan setting for the dying and sick. The nurse engaged in the usual small talk with the man in the bed before switching on the tv set for him. It had jumped to one of those odd financial channels that he never watched. He pointed the remote to change back to the snooker when the face on the screen caught his eye. He slowly dropped his hand to the side of the bed and left the same station on. It was him, it was definitely him they were talking about. *Matt Cunningham, the leader of Blackbaron technologies has announced he will retire next year. The company has agreed on a substantive remuneration package for the man who has led the Blackbaron Group through a difficult operating period in the last few years.* And there was his smiling face, beaming out from the TV set. Meanwhile, the large sick man in the bed looked on with a mixture of envy and hatred. It was as if someone had invented an inverted mirror that reflected the exact opposite of what he had become.

It would be a further few months before he was finally discharged from the hospital and allowed to go back home to his small flat in Kilmarnock. His drinking friends and nearby relatives had mostly abandoned him. A few had come to visit at the start but gradually their feeling of guilt had evaporated, and they no longer made the effort. It was time for him to change his life. He still had all his limbs and had lost 6 stone during his three months stay in the hospital. Money was tight, in fact, he was skint. Yes, the point had arrived, he had no choice. He would give up his flat and move down to Liverpool to stay with his mother. That would give him a base to work on a little idea that was forming in his head. Maybe things were looking up for the big guy after all.

(2014)

It was 2 pm and we had only 30 miles to go until arrival in Liverpool. We had pulled into the last service area on the M6 at Charnock Richard before taking the M58 and the last few miles to Sefton Street. V had not stipulated were in Liverpool they wanted us to go to, but the scene of our crime seemed to fit the occasion. I was trying to waste time rather than arrive too early. Almost as if I could foresee that the end was coming. We finished our coffees and headed out into the car park and the biting cold. 'Where is your girlfriend?' The Suit spoke the words without looking at me.

'She is not my fucking girlfriend Charlie, as you know damn well.' I stopped and looked back at the service area. Roni was like a cat, beside you one minute and the next she would disappear.

'Where the fuck has, she gone now?' I sighed with

impatience and started to walk back the way I had come. The Suit continued to the car. Who could blame him, it was like Siberia with the wind and swirling specs of snow biting into your skin. Just as I was about to push the glass doors open, Roni re-appeared, all smiles in her flowery Wellingtons.

'What the fuck Roni, can you stop disappearing every few fucking minutes. You are giving me the fear.' She shuffled up beside me and put her arm into mine.

'Thank fuck we never did stick together Matt. We have only been back together for five minutes and you sound like my fucking husband.'

We made it back to the car, the heater was blasting away making the inside feel homely and secure. The Suit drove carefully out towards the exit road. I stared ahead, there could be no more waiting, this was it now. Within a few hours, it would be all over. Either a fresh start or the end of everything. Two hands appeared from the back of the car holding a large box of chocolates, a road atlas and three packets of cheap writing pens. 'Anyone hungry or need to write a letter?'

'Where the fuck did you get that stuff, Roni. I thought you had no money left.' She laughed and I knew straight away that she was up to her usual tricks.

'Fucking hell Roni, are you insane. We need to get to Liverpool, you are going to get us arrested. Do you not care about fucking anything?' For the first time since she had belted me with the flower pot, I was genuinely annoyed with her. The last thing we needed was to attract trouble and miss our appointment with V. And then right on cue as if to prove my point, The Suit spoke.

'Uh-oh. We have trouble behind us.' We had almost made the start of the slip road when the traffic police car behind flashed its lights. I bowed my head in despair, this was it. A shoplifter, two murderers, a gun, and a fucking briefcase with 250k in it. We were done for now. They would throw the book at us. I watched as one of the policemen put on his yellow coat and walked up to the car. He rattled on the window for The Suit to open it. I just wanted to put my hands up and tell him to throw on the cuffs. At Least I would get a break from the two fucking lunatics I had got in tow with.

'It is you, I told George it was you. I saw you getting into the car and said to George, it's him for sure... Charles Cameron Ilderton well I never... You don't recognise me, do you?' The Suit looked perplexed and then slowly the dawn of recognition shone in his eyes.

'Cameron Jolley, Oh my god, it's little Cameron Jolley. That is uncanny, I was just texting your dad Carter only yesterday. Oh wow, Cameron, how are you? Fucking Jesus, the last time I saw you, it must be ten years ago, you had just left school.' Cameron extended his arm through the window and the two men shook hands vigorously.

'Yes, I followed my dad into the police force.' He laughed heartily before continuing.

'Not that dad was a good example. How the hell are you, Charlie? I always used to love it when you came to visit, you were such a good laugh. Where are you off to?'

'Oh, we are just on a little trip to catch up with some old friends. This is Matt and his girlfriend...' He did not get a chance to finish his sentence before Roni popped her head forward, all windswept curls and smiles.

'Bettina Jesmond, nice to meet you officer. I have always fantasised about meeting a handsome young man in a uniform. Are you married?' I sat in the passenger seat and inwardly sighed. *Was this woman for real?* Cameron laughed and taking Roni's extended hand he made a mock attempt to kiss it.

'And it is lovely to meet you as well Miss Jesmond. Your boyfriend is one very lucky guy. I hope he treats you like an angel?' I sat there saying nothing while feeling like an extra in a movie as the stars chatted each other up.

'Oh yes, don't worry about that officer. Matt treats me like a fucking princess. Why only yesterday he bought me a lovely pair of Wellington boots for £3.99.' Cameron gave me a glance as though to say, *wow what a gent.*

'Look I better get back into the car, it is freezing out here. I will tell dad I met you. Charlie, keep in touch with him, he thinks a lot of you. I live in Preston now with my partner Sally, she is expecting. The M6 from Carlisle to here is my patch. You would not believe some of the rogues you meet on this motorway, that's why it is nice to meet some normal people.' I silently prayed that Roni would not say anything else and we could escape from what could have been a tight call.

'I will do Cameron, regards to Sally and baby Jolley when he or she arrives. I promise to go and see your dad when I get back from this trip. Take care young man.' Cameron continued to ignore me and stretched his head to stare into the back of the car at Roni.

'Nice to meet you, Miss Jesmond. And I can assure you that if I was not married, I would defiantly take you up on that fantasy.' He smiled and then winked at her.

'Nice to meet you officer. Don't be too sure about us being normal people though. My silent boyfriend Matt in the front seat is a gun runner and I am a full-time shoplifter. Charlie is just kidding you on, he is a bounty hunter and is taking us back to Glasgow to get the reward.' Cameron gave a good hearty laugh before waving and running back to the warm Police car.

'Phew that was a close shave,' said The Suit. 'A lovely boy that Cameron, takes after his dad Carter Jolley, except he probably works harder than his old feller did. Mind you, his dad never did a stroke of real Police work in his life so that would not be too hard.' I turned around and looked at Roni.

'Gunrunner and a fucking shoplifter?' She tweaked my nose between her outstretched fingers.

'Stick with me, Matt. I will keep you right. It is not what you say but how you say it. If that copper had taken a closer look at you shitting yourself, we would have all been fucked. I was just making sure he did not get suspicious. Here, have a chocolate and calm down you big fucking girl.' I turned back to face the front, she was right. Roni in her own way was looking after me, she was no fool. She was a fucking nuts though.

(2009)

Roni only served 7 of the 11-year sentence she received for the murder of Giulio. I suppose it was a case of mitigating circumstances. Maybe they thought of it as diminished responsibility due to her alcoholism and his violent past. If you ask for my opinion though, I would have to be honest with you. I reckon they just decided to kick Roni back across the sea to Scotland to make way for an Italian nutcase. *Why the fuck should we pay to keep a scrounging British murderer in luxury when we could be looking after our own criminals in jail.* To be fair to Roni, the prison was a hell hole and she did behave immaculately. She probably sweet talked them into reducing her sentence while at the same time knocking out some 20 stone Italian woman in a fight. I think I already mentioned that they make them tough in Kilmarnock.

It would have been nice to think that the little lady from Scotland would come home, settle down and get her life into order. It was not to be though, Roni had not yet reached her nadir. That was still to come. I know it is hard to believe but she still had a long way to fall yet. On returning from Italy Roni moved in with her aging mother. The rumour mill had her down as a killer and most of Roni's old friends and family shunned the convicted murderer despite the circumstances. Jessie Paterson was old and frail by the time her daughter came back, and Roni tried to make it up by becoming her mother's carer. But the drinking restarted despite all the promises she had made to herself. Very soon each night was spent drifting into oblivion once her mother had fallen asleep.

Jesse passed away within six months of Roni coming home. Even though it was a short period and Roni's alcoholism sometimes came between them, it was a happy time. That tight bond that exists between a child and a mother remained firm. No matter what her daughter had done in the past, Jesse loved her without reservation. Roni enjoyed looking after her mum and taking care of the old lady in the final months of Jesse's life. Of course, Roni grieved after the funeral but very soon she was back sitting in the pub wasting her life away with the other afternoon drinkers and misfits.

It was a damp Tuesday afternoon when it all kicked off. It would be around 2pm, the drinks had been flowing since opening time at 11 that morning. Like the rest of the gang, Roni had drifted in before midday. Money was tight but despite being in her late forties she still maintained her looks as well as the charm to be able to cadge drinks from friends and casual acquaintances. The usual crowd was in. Benni the Fox, Copper Lamp Bill, Teflon Tony, Old Annie Leather Face, Marco Gob Shite, even Tam Empty Pockets had made it out. They all had nicknames, mostly given by Roni. She herself was known as Roni Rosie Cheeks. Some said it was because her face would flush when she drank. Others thought it was because she still had a trim bottom that wiggled in her jeans when she very occasionally went to the bar to buy a round. Anyway, back to that Tuesday afternoon I was telling you about.

Four men walked through the door. They were not complete strangers although they did not belong with the usual afternoon crew. One of them ordered the pints while the other three sat down close to the gang. A few drunken words of greeting and banter were exchanged between the two groups. At first, Roni did not pay any attention as she was caught up in a discussion with Annie Leather Face regarding who was better looking, Teflon Tony or Copper Lamp Bill. The two men being discussed listened intently, both hoping that Roni rather than Leather Face would consider them as the best catch.

'Ah reckon Teflon Tony wuz a reet fucking looker when he wuz a boy.' Annie snorted with laughter as she pointed at Tony while making the remark. Almost as though he needed to be reminded that was his name.

'Ah wuz a fucking good lookin guy when a wuz younger Annie, an am still a fucking good-looking guy the noo. Ye want tae gie me a chance tae show ye what ah can still dae Annie?' The ensemble broke out in laughter at the awful thought of Annie Leather Face and Teflon Tony doing anything other than drink.

'Get your brains back in your pants and behave yourself, Tony.' The usual put down from Roni had the group laughing even harder.

'So, come on Rosie Cheeks, who is the best lookin, me or Teflon?' But Roni was no longer listening to the words from Copper Lamp Bill. She had picked up on one of the new arrivals talking. It was his voice rather than the words that sounded familiar. Roni stared at the man, a very large figure with long white greasy hair. His large stomach protruding like a waterfall over his jeans. A black t-shirt with hundreds of white dandruff specs covering the shoulders. The folds of skin compressed under his chin like closely stacked shelves. It was a face she knew or had known. It was just that someone had painted the face onto a completely different body. And then realisation dawned on the two of them. A meeting of two old adversaries from the past, each eyeing the other up like boxers waiting for the referee to allow the first round to start.

Roni was thinking, *oh my God it is him. Tobi the fucking Virgin. Christ, he was no looker in the seventies, and he has sure not improved since then.* Meanwhile, the Virgin was thinking, *oh my God it is her. Roni fucking Paterson. She was a cute little bitch in the seventies and she still looks hot.*

That's the problem with drinking and being drunk. The boundaries between love and hate can suddenly converge and then cross over into each other. Two people who despise one another can drink their way to intimacy while another two who love each other can end up with one of them dead. And that is what happened with Tobi the Virgin and Roni. Despite initially being wary of one another they soon ended up talking and laughing while recalling their brief stint together in the punk band Social Decline. Roni enjoyed remembering the laughs they had with Matt and Calum. The difference being Tobi was not an alcoholic and his size meant he could drink the diminutive Roni under the table and still be in control. Despite being societies rejects, the gang looked after their own. Annie Leather Face, Teflon, and even Copper Lamp watched with growing concern as Big Tobi plied Roni with drink after drink. When Roni staggered to her feet and Tobi helped her put on her coat, they tried to intervene.

'Where the fuck are you gaun Rosie Cheeks? It is only 6 o'clock, too early to call it a day.' Annie asked the question of Roni but looked at Tobi as she said it.

'Fuckin goin to Moley's Bar for another drink. Ma pal Tobi here is gonna buy me another drink. We are celebrating old times, used tae be in a band together. This is Tobi, ma old mate. We used tae be in a band. Did a tell ye we used to play n a band together?' It was rare for Roni to be so pissed that she could hardly talk. She swayed from side to side as she staggered out with Tobi holding onto her arm to keep her from falling over. The gang watched the two of them disappear out of the door. The massive frame of big Tobi seemed to envelop little Rosie Cheeks. It was as though his bulk was sucking her tiny body into his like a giant tarantula. Annie was the first to speak as the door closed behind the unlikely couple.

'Ah fuckin hate that big fat bastard Tobi Kingston. He

left years ago, fancied himself as some kinda fucking rock star. Fat fucking bastard. Ah dinnae like Roni going aff wi him, the fat fuck.' It was Benni the Fox who answered her.

'Ach Rosie Cheeks will eat the fat fucker alive. Stop fucking worrying aboot her ye daft auld woman. Is it no time ye bought a fucking roond Annie?' The gang soon forgot about Rosie Cheeks as the drink continued to flow. Well most of them did, Annie Leather Face still fretted about her little friend even though she still carried on sipping her vodka.

The odd couple staggered into Moley's but after just two drinks the barman asked them to leave. He knew Roni and liked her, but it was obvious that she was beyond drunk and had now arrived at almost incapable.

'Come back to my place Roni. I have some great malt whisky, we can continue talking about the good old days.' By now Roni was starting to feel sick. She was close to passing out but was still wise enough to know that The Virgin had only one thing on his mind. She had only put up with his company because he had bought her drink and she enjoyed talking about Matt and the old days. She looked at the slobbering big hulk sitting opposite her and thought about Matt. It was strange how she would occasionally reminisce about a boy she had not seen for 35 years. What is it they say about never forgetting your first love? Or was it because she and Matt had a bond, something that would always hold them together no matter how far apart they were. Birkbys blood was like a glue that would not allow them to separate no matter how hard they tried. She might have killed Giulio, but she had helped Matt murder an innocent shopkeeper. In her eyes, there was a difference. Roni threw up, all over the table in Moley's Bar and then toppled off her seat before passing out.

Roni had been through countless drunken horrors in her life. Christ, she had even spent 7 years in a tough Italian jail as well as watching her own mother die. Nothing would or could ever have prepared her for this. The problem was that she was so drunk that evening that only vague snapshots of the nightmare came back. Anger, revulsion, and reality fused together so that she could not think straight without breaking down or flying into a rage. She remembered being in such a mess that she relied on Tobi to get her home. At first, they had talked, he seemed concerned and had even tried to get her to drink some water. She was sure they had talked about Matt and then she had cried as the alcohol and emotion loosened her tongue. Did she tell Tobi about what happened after they left Liverpool and went their separate ways?

He was on top of her ripping her clothes, pawing like a dirty big animal at her flesh. Even in her drunken state little Roni made a brave attempt to fight the large hulk of a man off. Eventually, she gave up and allowed her mind if not her body to drift into oblivion. It had been the only way to survive. He did not care about her as a human being, to him she was a filthy drunk. The lowest of the low, there for the taking and getting what she deserved. Something to be used for his pleasure and then discarded half-clothed on the floor. Roni remembered making one final plea, one last desperate attempt to save herself from the repulsive sweating man who used her like a ragdoll. Did he really do that? Did he laugh in her face as he mauled her? Whether her drink-addled brain added embellishments to the nightmare mattered not one bit. What happened, happened and Roni would carry the scars for the rest of her life.

Maybe that was the day she really changed. The first move was to get as far away from Kilmarnock as possible. She had to make sure she would never see him again. Never have to take the risk of letting him leer across the street at her as they walked past each other. What else could she do? Roni was well known as a drunk, a low life. If she had reported what happened, they would have ridiculed her. *What, Roni Paterson. That bam pot who murdered her boyfriend in Italy? That nutjob who has been arrested for being drunk and disorderly countless times in the town centre? Rape, are you fucking serious? Tell her to go and sober up.*

Roni had difficulty selling her mother's house. The small building was in poor condition and she had little money to fix it up. It took some time but eventually, she managed to get rid of it and was able to purchase the equally run-down cottage in remote Bendrennon. It was as if the only way she could try to wash that animal Kingston from her body was to be somewhere he would never be able to find her. Some of her old friends knew she was going and were sad to see her leave. Annie Leather Face even promised to write but Roni was not convinced that Annie could write. She did not expect a letter anytime soon. A few of the gang including Annie, Copper Lamp and Teflon even turned up at Kilmarnock train station to see her leave. It was a good job she got the early train though as it was unlikely, they would have been there once opening time came at the pub.

'Al miss wee Rosie cheeks for sure.' Teflon spoke the words in a wistful tone, as though he considered himself to be some sort of poet.

'Ach fucking shut it, the only thing you will miss is eying up wee Rosie cheeks arse when she goes up to the bar.' Annie ignored the comment from Copper Lamp before adding her own poignant observation as the train departed.

'Something happened that night. It wis that big fat bastard Tobi Fucking Kingston. Ah fuckin telt ye, he wiz up tae no good. Wee Rosie wis never the same after that night. It was fucking him am tellin yese.'

Roni glanced out of the window and waved as the train moved towards the end of the platform. It was too late; the three drinkers had already left to make the short walk to the pub and the opening drinks of the day.

Now you might have thought that in a perfect world Roni would have seen the light this time and started her new life as a sober woman. But as you already know it did not quite work out that way. I think it would only be fair that we cut her some slack though and remember what she had been through. Maybe she needed to keep on drinking to help her forget, blank out the memory of what happened. It would take a few more years of court appearances, fights and drinking the dregs out of near-empty bottles before Roni finally changed her life.

Look, I am no expert on alcoholism even though I like a drink or two. But I swear to God this is what happened. It really was as simple as this, it can happen. Yes, I know it is unusual and very rare but not impossible. One morning Roni woke half-dressed on the bed in the cold dilapidated cottage at Bendrennon. She was surrounded by her own vomit and empty vodka bottles lay strewn across the floor. She knew there would be nothing left, and it would be a case of draining the dregs out of the near empty containers until she could buy more alcohol. She slid off the bed and onto the floor, her knee crashing into one of the bottles on the filthy carpet. Roni went to push it away and was surprised to find it was still half full. She picked it up and stared with disbelief at the white liquid floating about inside. And then to her amazement and no doubt our surprise, she flung it at the wall. The glass smashed into a million tiny pieces sending the contents slithering and dripping down towards the floor.

I am not going to try and convince you that Roni simply walked away from years of drinking. It was not as easy as that. While in prison she had been forced to stop, this time she had to do it all by herself. But the little woman from Kilmarnock proved us all wrong. She did stop and she did pull herself together. I told you they make them tough in that town. And maybe Roni would have gone on planting her pots and tending the little house and garden, but it was not to be. The envelope arrived that day with the note and the words written in back ink.

A murderer must always pay the price in the long run. V

The difference between Roni and her first love Matt? Well, while he was reading his blackmail note and trembling in his expensive leather shoes. She was putting her old Wellington boots on and thinking about revenge. But not until she got a new pair of wellies, first things first.

Annie Leather Face (1948-2010)

Asleep on a bench, covered by old blankets

Unmoving, not a sound in the bleak icy cold

Two plastic bags containing all her life

Kilmarnock's own Annie Leather Face, every line a tale untold, every crease a broken promise

Only the weather-stained nose and crimson eyes open to the biting wind

The smell of urine and stale alcohol

A wisp of tobacco smoke embedded in every pore

Two plastic bags gripped so tight

Kilmarnock's own Annie Leather Face, once a mother, once a child

Spare not your grief or sympathy

Give not your sermon to float on the cruel wind

The two plastic bags are none of your business

But if you have some spare change that burdens your pocket

Kilmarnock's own Annie Leather Face will bless you for her next drink.t

An empty bench now able to sparkle with frost

Breeze-blown bags shuffle against the kerb

We all live and die to make our mark

You may stroll past with your head held high

But I know Kilmarnock's own Annie Leather Face will be missed more than you.

CHAPTER EIGHT:
THE EXPLODING
MAN

(2014)

After the meeting with the jolly policeman, we made it to Liverpool without further incident. As we neared the scene of our crime all three of the car's occupants became silent. Even The Suit seemed to be lost in his own thoughts. Maybe he was just dreaming about what he would spend his 200k on when this was all over? Roni too said nothing. It was a change to see her so withdrawn when previously she had seemed indifferent to our past and Birkby. I just assumed that was the only way she could cope with it, but maybe now we were close, she too could feel our history coming back to envelop us with guilt.

The Suit found his way to Sefton Street, or should I say, Glenda, the satnav found her way. We parked in an empty space on the vaguely familiar road. It was 5.30 in the afternoon, thirty minutes until V made contact to let me know if I had a future or not. I had the 250k in cash, that was my limit. I would pay more if forced to, but I was sure as hell going to barter for V's silence. This whole fuck up had now cost me 450k including the money for my accountant, The Suit, and the gun. I also planned to give Roni something once this was all over. Bloody hell, at this rate my Blackbaron pay off would soon be gone. Even Cara might notice the rate I was throwing our money away. It would all be worth it though. *Half a million to buy my way back to normality*. I repeated the words over in my head but somehow was still not convinced.

I could not stand waiting in silence any longer. 'Do you recognise anywhere Roni? I mean can you remember were Birkby's shop might have been?' The buildings in the run-down street looked as though they would have been the same ones from the seventies. The once affluent semi-detached houses now looked as though they had been turned into student flats. A lot of young university types could be seen walking along the pavements. The few retail outlets now housed mostly fast food takeaways with the occasional charity shop or bookies making an appearance.

'No, sorry Matt. It all looks the same to me. I don't

want to see the shop anyway. What is the point? Stop torturing yourself and sit still will you man.'

'Fuck this, I am going for a walk. I have my phone for when V calls anyway.'

I left the two of them sitting silently in the car and walked along Sefton Street. It was a long broad avenue with the same buildings on repeat. It reminded me of one of those streets you used to see in seventies cartoons like Tom and Jerry. They would be running along, and the same four houses would continually pass by. I think it was to save them having to draw another million cards, so they just re-used the same set repeatedly. They probably assumed that kids like me did not notice, but we did. Well I did, there was fuck all else to do in the seventies, so you tended to pay more attention to shite. Remember this was long before laptops, tablets, handsets, pc games, and the internet. The only tablets we got were the ones you took to cure a hangover.

I must apologise for twittering on, I was nervous. Time seemed to have stopped while I waited for the call. And then I saw it. I knew straight away that it was his shop. It was boarded up. Steel panels had been placed across the large glass frontage. The door was barred with a high metal gate about three feet in front of it. The gap between the gate and the door was filled with rubbish, empty bottles, old newspapers and discarded food containers. The sign above the shop read, Ali's PC Repairs and Electrics. Well, I assumed that is what is said, the last part of the plastic sign had fallen off so now it read, Ali's PC Repairs and Elect. Maybe he fixed computers and then asked you to vote for him, probably not. So, it must have meant to say Electrics. But I digress, I could not have given a fuck about Ali and what he did or used to do. It was the letters the missing part of the sign had exposed underneath that held my frozen stare. Barely readable with the passage of more than 35 years I could just make out the grimy weather-beaten letters that said, *ries*. If I had been able to pull the rest of the sign down there would be little doubt that the words, Birkby & Son General Groceries would appear. The full name pointing back at me. It might have well just said, Birkby, murdered by you.

The bloody phone buzzed and I damn near shat myself. Christ, I had got so lost in my past that six o'clock had arrived like an express train. My hands were shaking as I moved the handset to my ear. 'Hello.' I wanted to say hello you bastard, but my management negotiation skills had kicked in.

'Well hello Mr. Cunningham, or is it ok to call you Matt?' At last V was an entity. The voice was male. He sounded hoarse, I could tell he was old.

'You can call me what the fuck you want. Just tell me how much your blood money is going to be, and we can finish this once and for all.'

'Blood money Matt? How ironic you should accuse me of taking blood money. You are the one with blood on your hands, not me.' The voice sounded vaguely familiar. Someone from a long-forgotten past.

'Ok. Who are you and more importantly what do you want?'

'For now, you can keep calling me V. I have decided what I want, in fact, I have decided on a few things. Have you brought that tramp Paterson with you, as I told you too?'

'Roni is with me, yes.'

'Good, good. Ok, this is what I want from you Mr big shot corporation Matt.' I wondered why he sounded so bitter. Whoever he was, I must have crossed him somehow during my life.

'In thirty minutes, I will text you my current address and you will come with Roni. Just the two of you, any double crossing and trust me, you will pay.' This was the last thing I had expected, why would V expose who he was? It did not make sense.

'Ok, and then what?'

'Oh, yes, of course, I almost forgot. I think 250k should be enough to keep me both happy and quiet.' *Fuck me*, I thought. Well, no I don't mean fuck me literally. I mean it as in fuck me, that is exactly the price I was willing to pay. Why am I telling you this, you fucking know what I mean? I think I was beginning to lose it. I was happy that V had asked for the exact amount I was willing to give him. It saved me from going to the bank again or having to contact that money grabbing accountant of mine. No wonder I ended up as a good manager, I could even work out a cost-effective price between a murderer and a blackmailer. Fuck me, oh no, here we go again.

'250k, how the hell do you expect me to find that amount of money? Anyway, how do I know that you won't come back asking for more?' The voice on the other end of the phone burst into hoarse laughter followed by a coughing fit. It took him at least another thirty seconds to be able to answer me.

'You can afford 250k Cunningham, don't give me that

bullshit. I reckon you are smart enough to already have the cash with you. You received a £1.5 million cash pay off from Blackbaron, it was in the press release. Add that to your fucking massive pension and I am giving you a fucking bargain. In fact, Cunningham, you are starting to piss me off, why don't we just forget the cash, I shall call the police, tell them what I know. Fuck you and your little tramp Paterson.'

'No, no V. I am sorry. 250k is fine, I will pay it. I just want this over with.' I was grovelling, for the first time in years. Most had to grovel to me. People wanting promotions, jobs, companies wanting contracts with Blackbaron. All had to come cap in hand to the great Matt Cunningham and now here I was. Almost on my knees, kissing arse, pleading to be given a reprieve.

'I will text you my address as I said. You and Paterson, alone. We will do the deal and that will be it over. I will not be back for more. But just in case you try to be clever, I have engineered a little safety net. A letter going into every detail about you and Birkby is sitting on the bed in a motel. The cleaners will come to do the room tomorrow morning. I will give you the key when I see you, but you will only get the address by text once I have the money and we have said our goodbyes.' He started laughing again, followed by another coughing fit. I had to admit, he had planned this well. Even down to the last detail of being able to humiliate me to my face. The phone went dead, and I started to walk back to the car. I could feel the ghost of Birkby watching me as I trudged with my head bowed along the wet street.

We dropped The Suit off at the first hotel we passed on the way to Flat 27A Colby Terrace. It meant me driving the hire car without insurance but by now I did not care. Glenda the Satnav told us it was only a 10-minute journey. As promised, the text from V had arrived. Ilderton stepped out of the car and went into the boot to get his bag. I could sense that he was disappointed to be getting dumped just as the finale was arriving. We had agreed, well I had told them that we would spend the night in Liverpool once the deal was done. Christ I might even have a drink to celebrate my freedom if everything went ok. I just hoped that the motel V had placed the letter in would not be too far away. I suppose it would have made sense to stay in the place I would need to drive to, but I felt obliged to give Ilderton something to do.

'Two rooms or three Matt?' The Suit still liked to be a smart arse even in a moment of crisis.

'Get as many rooms as you fucking want. We will be

back once I have retrieved the letter from the motel. I will call if things go wrong. Other than that, get me a beer lined up on the bar.'

'Your wish is my command, Sir.' He was talking to himself as I was already in second gear and heading with Roni to our rendezvous with V.

'It is strange Roni. I thought I recognised his voice, even though it was on the phone. He sort of sounded familiar.' Roni just stared ahead. She was acting odd, I mean odder than she usually did. She was always so relaxed, at ease with the world. She seemed tense for the first time since I had met her at Bedrennon.

'Are you ok Roni? Look I know this is tough for you as well. It will soon be over.' She glanced sideways at me.

'Do you think so, Matt. Do you think it really will be over?' I did not like her reply. It was as though she knew more about all this than I did.

'How much is in the black briefcase Matt?' It was the first time she had mentioned it, but I knew she had watched me carry the bag to the car that morning.

'250,000 pounds, Roni. But it does not matter. It could be 5 pounds or 5 million pounds, it means nothing if it allows us to walk away.' She sighed before replying.

'You don't need to pay him, Matt. You know that don't you?' I looked at her, feeling confused. I had no time for Roni's abstraction. We had a deal to do, a project to close out. I ignored her comment and continued driving.

At the next junction turn left and then in one hundred yards, turn left again. You will arrive at your destination. Glenda the Satnav spoke the words as though she was the only normal person left in the world. It was one of those cheaply built little estates, small white flats crowded around each other in separate little buildings. Totally none descript. Maybe if I had been writing a book, I would have made V live in some sort of windswept Gothic mansion on the Cornish coast. But I am telling you what really happened, and the truth was my tormentor lived in a little suburban estate full of students and old people. There was a bus stop outside the entrance to V's three-story block of flats. The plastic canopy had the words, *Mavis loves cock* spray painted over it. Attached to a post was an overflowing bin that had been partially set on fire some time ago. Black plastic had frozen into grotesque gnarled shapes down the front but on the plus side, it had melted into the rubbish it still held tightly. Seeing the bin was full, people had placed their crap around it. Not quite a good citizen but not a bad one either.

If they had been the latter, then they would no doubt have chucked the stuff in the street. I like a bit of respect, just a touch. It shows some class at least.

We stepped out of the car and walked together towards the shared entrance. I clutched the case with the blood money tucked inside it. Roni took her reading glasses out of the shopping bag that held her life and pressed the button marked Flat 27A. No answer, she pressed again. 'Come on you fucker.' Hearing my companion spit the words out unnerved me.

'Roni, listen to me.' She turned around and looked into my eyes. I thought they looked sad, as though she knew the end was near.

'What is it, Matt?'

'Roni, I can't afford any fuck up here. The last thing I need is for you to be a hero and belt him with a flower pot. We need to be discrete, get this over with. Give him the money, I will pay him. You have nothing to lose and everything to gain. We hand over the case to him and walk away, free agents.' She shook her head and pressed the intercom again.

'Yes, free agents, whatever you say Matt. We all walk away, off to happy land.' The sarcasm in her voice was unnerving. But I had no time to react, the buzzer went, and we were allowed into the shared hallway. A few more steps and we stood at the door of 27A. It was open, waiting for us to enter.

It looked like a bachelor flat, sparsely furnished. A place to survive rather than live in. An atmosphere of neglect and apathy mingling with the smell of fried cooking and dampness. We edged through the hallway with me leading. I pushed what I assumed to be the living room door and entered, feeling like a schoolboy who had come to see the headmaster. He was a large man. You could see he had once been larger, folds of skin running down his neck and bulging out of his black t-shirt. He was sitting in an armchair, two cases on the floor beside him. His walking stick held in his hand. Ready to do the deal and move off to another life.

'Hello Matt, it has been a long time.' The face was familiar, even though it had sunk into the fat surrounding his head. But recognition was coming, my mind was racing ahead, trying to piece the last bits of the jigsaw into place.

'Ahh, and the lovely little Roni Paterson. I bet you are delighted to see me again, although you probably don't remember much of our last rendezvous.' He started laughing and then choking before continuing. 'Do you still like to drink yourself into bed Paterson?'

I could see her go for him, just the slightest move but I knew it was coming. I had been ready for it. As Roni went to attack, I grabbed her in a straitjacket hold. Christ, for a small woman she was bloody strong when she was angry. It took all my strength to hold onto her. Maybe I should have let her go, she would have ripped him to bits.

'You fucking fat bastard Kingston, you dirty stinking fat fucking bastard.' The name finally pulled it all together for me. It was him, our band leader. Tobi fucking Kingston, the Virgin. He was off his seat now, waddling towards Roni, the walking stick raised above his head ready to strike. I swung her around with one arm and used the other to fend off the blow aimed at her head.

'Jesus Christ, will you two calm down.' I held tightly onto Roni and steered her out into the hall.

'Get back in the car Roni, do as I fucking tell you.' I pushed her towards the exit, but she still spun back around to face me.

'You don't fucking understand Matt, you just don't get it.'

'Don't get what Roni? For Christ sake, this is almost over. It is just fucking money; will you leave me to sort this out.'

Suddenly she seemed to calm down. It unnerved me, almost as though a mist had descended to surround her. One that spoke of a different solution. I was surprised to see her meekly walk off, the shared entrance door slamming behind her. Within seconds I had returned to the living room that held the angry fat guy.

'Ok Tobi, let us not prolong this any longer. I have the 250k here, just get out of my life and Roni's as well. Take your money and go. Just tell me one thing, why? What have you got against me? Surely to fuck you are not still pissed about that stupid fucking concert we screwed up.' He was back in his chair, sweat running down his face, the black t-shirt damp from the exertion of raising his walking stick.

'I met that little cow Paterson a few years back. She can't hold her drink or her mouth. She told me about the Birkby thing. Then last year I saw you on TV, talking about how successful you had become. You a fucking murderer and life gives you a fortune while I have nothing and yet never harmed a soul.' His beady eyes peered at me through the overlapping skin with contempt and hatred.'

'How did you find where Roni lived and get my address? In fact, you even came into my work.'

'It was easy.' He spoke the words with utter contempt. 'That little cow told her filthy drinking buddies where she was moving too. They can't hold their tongues either. I paid a mate to visit your work. The prick was supposed to leave another note, but he panicked and left. I got him to follow you home one night. That is how I found out where you live. Nice big fucking house Cunningham.'

'Ok, Tobi, Ok. But Roni has nothing, why make her suffer as well. She does not deserve all this.' He laughed and started to choke causing more sweat to run in beads down his face and neck.

'She is a fucking nobody, even I got a shot of her. A dirty drunken floozy who will have anyone,' It was strange how I had been able to treat this whole thing as a project. Something to be finished and then paid for. But the way he spoke about Roni was like a knife being twisted in my heart. I stormed forward and grabbed him by the throat.

'Kingston, take my fucking money but leave her out of it.' He stumbled to his feet again and used his weight to push me away.

'I don't give a fuck about your little tramp. Keep her, you deserve each other.'

I wanted to kill him now, but we were so close to

finishing all this. I calmed down, used my management skills. Restarted the negotiation. *Finish this Matt, close it out, do it for the company. Regain the middle ground. Pay him off and close out the project.*

We did the deal, I handed the case over. He did not even open it, so sure was he of having played the game and won. The Virgin gave me the key to the motel room. I pleaded with him to tell me the address, but he would not budge. I knew he would send it within an hour as agreed though. If he screwed me now and the Birkby thing blew up in my face, then the fat guy was coming down as well. The fact that he had set up the blackmail and held back what he knew would mean prison for him too. I would like to say we shook hands at the completion of the project, but the hatred was mutual. I turned to walk out of his stinking little hovel but turned around to say my last words.

'Kingston. Let me be clear on one thing. If you ever cross my path again, I will kill you before they can send me to prison.' He knew I meant it. This was our one and only chance to walk away from each other for good.

'I won't be back. I don't need any more money than this. You can keep the rest, Cunningham. I won't snitch on your little murder.' I walked back into the room and knelt, my face just inches from his.

'It will not be because of Birkby that I will find you Kingston.' Maybe, just maybe I could see a flicker of fear in his bloodshot eyes.

'Tough guy aye Cunningham. Go on them, tell me why?'

'I don't know exactly what you did to Roni or what your involvement was with her. Just be glad I don't know because if I did then I would not be leaving this room until you were dead.' We stared at each other for a few seconds longer and then I left. Free at last, it was over.

She sat silently in the car beside me as we left the horror of the past few weeks behind. I felt elated, as though I had control of my life back at last. Roni seemed less jubilant, lost in thought.

'Are you ok Roni?' I tried to squeeze her arm in an act of affection. Even that felt wrong now, that simple touch. The two people who had shared everything were now strangers again.

'Look, Roni, I will take you back to Bendrennon tomorrow. I will sort out your money problems, you will never have to worry again.' She turned and shook her head.

'Fuck off Matt.'

'Roni, what do you want me to say? We must get back to normal, this whole business is crazy. I have a wife and a daughter, you have your own life.'

'Fucking hell Matt, you really are so up your own arse. Do you always think everything is about you and what you want or think you want? Pull over here, I will walk back to the hotel. I need some fresh air, some space. I will catch up with you when you get back from finding the note.'

'I am sorry Roni, I really am. Sorry, I ever involved you in the first place and sorry you had to go back through all this.'

'Yes, I know Matt, I know.' I stopped the car and she pulled the door handle to open it.

'Let me get my bag out of the boot before you drive off.' Roni walked to the back of the motor and opened the lid. I could see her rummaging about in the rear-view mirror. She came back and looked into the car.

'I will see you back at the hotel.' She leaned in and kissed the side of my face.

'Thanks for protecting me lover boy. Maybe you would survive in prison after all.' She poked her finger in my nose and then walked away. The bulging plastic bag in her hand and the flowery Wellington boots on her feet. The odd thing is I can remember wondering why her bag looked so heavy?

A few minutes later the text arrived, and I was driving like a banshee towards Preston. The bastard had still left me work to do. An hour would see me at Horton Lodge Motel. I could get the note left on the bed, come back to Liverpool and sleep. It was almost over.

The plastic bag was not strong enough to hold the contents. Roni cursed as the handle finally stretched too far and ripped. She scooped the damaged container up into her hands and made it into a bundle. It was not far now. She had carefully watched the streets pass by for five minutes until demanding that Matt let her out to walk the rest of the way. A little corner shop lurched into view as she hurried along the road. It looked like every other little grocery store, no different to the one Birkby had owned all those years ago. Roni walked in and went straight up to the counter. 'Can I have two plastic bags please?' The Indian shopkeeper looked her up and down in surprise.

'Just two plastic bags madam, nothing else?'

'Yes, just two plastic bags, that is all.' She fiddled about with the damaged bag she already owned before finally producing ten pence to pay for her purchase. The shopkeeper watched in amusement as she walked to the doorway and then started transferring a few clothes, a hairbrush, and some make-up into one of the good bags. She then wrapped the ripped plastic around what was left inside and placed it into the second bag. Whatever it was seemed to be heavy, as though it was made of metal. The shopkeeper shrugged, he had seen stranger things than the little woman who had come in to spend ten pence. He liked her, he had no idea why, he just did.

'Take care madam, have a good evening.' Roni turned around and smiled at him.

'I intend to, thanks.'

It was getting close to seven o'clock and the light was fading. Roni walked back along the road she had left less than an hour ago. She read the label that said 27A but this time she pressed the buzzer for 27B. Her heart was beating fast, not because she was concerned about seeing him again. It was the fear that he might have already left. Taken the bag and the money and already started his new life. The door remained tightly closed so she pressed another few buttons randomly, all of them except 27A. Finally, the door clicked open, someone had released it without checking who it was. Roni crept quietly through the shared entrance to the door of his flat. Incredibly it was still slightly ajar, *did that mean he was already gone?* She tiptoed into the smelly damp hallway and slowly placed one of the bags on the floor. She then removed the small gun from the other bag.

'Who the fuck is there? Is that the taxi driver? Hello, who is there?' Roni could hear The Virgin shuffling to his feet. She wanted to scream with relief at the sound of his voice. She strode quickly forward and pushed the living room door open. He had sat back down, his large carcase moulded into the seat. A mass of sweat and blubber with two large cases and a small black one at his side. He looked at her in amazement and then laughed before following up with a coughing fit. She held the gun in her small hands and pointed it at his face.

'Paterson, are you fucking serious? Put the gun away, you shoot me and both you and lover boy are going to jail. Two murders, what are you some kind of fucking serial killer?' He was still half choking from laughing and coughing as he spluttered the words out. Roni moved within a few feet of him and stood perfectly still, the gun trained on his massive face.

'Three actually, when I kill you, Mr. Virgin. Did I never tell you that I killed my boyfriend in Italy as well?' She was smiling, all the hatred and resentment forming into a shard

of bright light that poured from her face. The moment she
had dreamed about, wept about, despised herself for, hated
everyone for, it had all come into focus during these last few
seconds. For the first time in years Tobi Kingston really saw,
really looked into another person's eyes and accepted that
the world did not just revolve around him. And suddenly he
knew fear, for a few seconds he even understood guilt and
remorse.

'Look, Roni. Come on, you were drunk, you came
onto me as much as I did to you. How about you come with
me, we could share the money. Look, I will even give you a
hundred grand if you just want to leave and take some cash.'
He was pleading now and maybe he might have got away
with it had he not mentioned the bit about Roni coming
onto him.

'You dirty fucking fat pig Kingston. Oh my God, no
matter how low I sank in life I would never come on to a
piece of shit like you.'

And then she simply took another few paces forward
and before The Virgin could blink, she pulled the trigger.
His face disintegrated and then exploded sending blood and
flesh splattering onto the back of the armchair and the walls.

The little lady had learned a lot during her time in that

Italian prison. She calmly wiped the handle of the gun on her dress before placing it in the dead man's hands and then went out into the hall. She hoped they might put it down to suicide but did not really care. Roni changed her clothes with the ones in the plastic bag and then walked out of the flat without looking back. If luck was on her side, then maybe no one would notice the little lady walking down the road with two shopping bags and a briefcase with 250,000 pounds in it. I told you the Kilmarnock girls are not to be messed with.

I had to admit, I might not like Tobi Kingston as a person, but he had style when it came to being a bastard. Not only had he scammed me for 250k, but he was even making me work for my freedom after I had paid him. Glenda the Satnav guided me around the last few turnings before I drove into the car park. The Neon sign shone above the entrance into the little motel. It was one of those square modern red brick office type buildings, maybe no more than 12 rooms on each of its two floors. Now you might be wondering why I am going into so much detail about the place rather than just getting on with finding the note Tobi the Bastard had left in the room. You see, that was the problem. He had sent me the name of the motel but not the number of the room. I had texted him back but as expected he ignored me. He was probably already on the way to his exotic new life in Jamaica or Sunderland to spend the money I had given him.

To my relief, there was no one at the small reception. It was probably only staffed at certain times. One of those cheap motels you can book on the internet and they send you a card to open the door to your room. I started on the ground floor going through each door to see if the little light would turn green and let me in. It was one of those moments in life where you say to yourself, *knowing my fucking luck it will be the last door I try.* But you know what? I was not even as lucky as that. I slipped the card into the reader at room number eleven just as it opened. A rather elderly lady shuffled out, took one look at me and screamed her fucking head off.

'S, S, Sorry. Calm down, I am really sorry. I seem to have got mixed up with my room. It must be the same one but the next floor. Really sorry.' To be honest, she had scared the shit out of me, I damn near wet my pants. I hurried off towards the flight of stairs hoping she would accept my explanation. I saw her shuffle as fast as she could towards the phone at the reception. I knew she had not been convinced at my explanation. Christ, she was about 90, what did she really think I was after? Maybe she thought I was going to steal her false teeth?'

I tried every fucking door on the next floor and nothing. That only left two explanations, either it was room 12 on the ground floor, the one I had left when Old Mother Hubbard confronted me. Or, it was one I had already tried, and it had not worked. Maybe the Virgin was playing one last trick on me? It proved to be the one room I had missed out, the very last of 24. How fucking unlucky can one person be? I was totally stressed out by the time I charged into the bedroom to look for the note. I was imagining police cars rushing towards Horton Lodge Motel, racing to arrest the granny grabber.

The note lay on the perfectly made bed. He had simply booked the room to allow him to leave the envelope. I picked it up with a sigh of relief and raced out towards the exit. Old Mother Hubbard was still standing in the reception. She turned around as I went to walk past, and she smiled. She had her teeth in so at least she must have known I was not intending to steal them. 'I hope you found your room young man?' I know it sounds ridiculous, but I felt flattered, no one had called me a *young man* in years.

'I did, thank you. I can only apologise for giving you such a fright.'

'Oh no, it is ok. You did startle me but when I saw your face, I could tell you were a trustworthy man. You don't get to my age without being able to read people and you are as honest as they come.' I smiled and thanked her while trying not to look guilty as I walked back to the car. And you know what? I opened the letter and inside was a drawing of a smiling face on a blank piece of paper. Under the sketch were the words, *Sucker*. He should have been a pantomime villain that Tobi Kingston. He had played me to the last, I almost wished him luck in his new life. 250k would buy a hell of a lot of donuts.

Roni finally arrived back at the hotel The Suit had booked the three of us into for the night. It had taken her more than an hour to walk back. She would have got a taxi but the loose change she had would hardly be enough to buy another plastic bag. She checked at reception what rooms Charles Cameron Ilderton had taken and headed up to the one he had reserved under her name. She went their first and dumped the bags as well as the case with the money in it before taking a shower. Within fifteen minutes she was knocking at the door of The Suit's room. 'Well hello gorgeous, you are back. How did it go, did you pay V off? Where is Matt?'

'Matt will be back shortly. Yes, it is all over.' She walked past him and sat uninvited on the chair beside the bed. The Suit could sense that this was a business visit rather than a social one.

'Well thank god that is all done with and we can all go home, eh gorgeous. Are you ok, what's up little lady?' Roni looked at him, her face emotionless. As though the words she was about to speak were all that mattered. She had no fear and cared only about one thing, the truth.

'Mr. Suit. You know, don't you?' Charlie fidgeted with his hair as he looked at her. He was not enjoying this, somehow the person he always thought of as being petite, cute and slightly crazy had suddenly become someone to be reckoned with. If truth be told, it could be said that he was afraid of her. Just for that moment, he recognised what she might be capable of.

'Know what Roni. What are you talking about?' She stood up and marched up to within a few feet of him. He towered over her, a big man.

'You lied to Matt about Birkby. Don't try and bullshit me, Mr. Suit, I am not a pushover like he is. You lied and now I want you to tell him the truth. Even if it means he takes the money back that he paid you, that is still the better option.' Charles Cameron Ilderton knew what the other option was but could not help but ask. You see he liked to talk.

'And option number two, little lady?' Roni laughed and stretched up onto her welly-booted toes. She kissed The Suit on his lips before speaking.

'Option number two is, I fucking blow your head off.' And then she walked towards the door before turning around to give one last instruction.

'Tell him tomorrow morning. He has been through a lot, let him have his rest tonight and you can tell him when he gets up. I am going to bed, I will see you in the morning. Goodnight Charlie.' She smiled at him and he smiled back. It was an acknowledgement that they would still be friends so long as he came clean and told the truth. And he had every intention of doing so because The Suit knew that Roni was deadly serious.

I parked the car in an empty space in the car park. It was finally all over, I felt so tired, more exhausted than relieved. It was time to start rebuilding my life. I pressed Cara's mobile number, it was dead. I could tell she had blocked me.

I phoned the house and it too was dead. I suppose I should have expected this, I had put her through hell. The best thing was to get home tomorrow and tell her the truth. But how would she react? If she knew about Birkby would she hand me in? I doubted it. Even if our marriage was over it would be a disaster if my past crime became known. I mean what would the neighbours say? The Pilates class would be horrified.

And then I started laughing, laughing at this whole damn fuck up. In just over a week I had gone from middle-class normality to sitting outside a hotel in Liverpool. 400,000 pounds worse off. But was I really? It was odd but the two people in the hotel, Roni and Charlie meant more to me now than anyone back home did, except of course for my daughter. The three of us had been through a lot together and they had stuck by me. Ok, I had paid The Suit but somehow, I felt he would have done it all for nothing. And Roni? Well maybe I would not admit it to myself, but I was in love with her, I suppose I always had been.

I went to my room and cleaned up. I wanted to start the process of returning to my old life, I even tried to call my best friend Eric but oddly, even his phone was not ringing. I would give Roni 100k, I knew she would not take it, but I was going to give her it anyway. Even if it meant buying her a new car or a house. I could not let her go back to rattling about for loose change.

There was no answer when I knocked on the door to Roni's room. The Suit was already down at the bar, so I joined him. He told me Roni was sleeping so I decided to leave her alone. She had been through a lot having to meet Tobi Kingston again. Best let her sleep it all off. We could talk in the morning. I told Charlie the whole story, explaining who V had turned out to be. For once he listened to me talking, in fact, he seemed unsettled. I suppose he had been through a lot as well. We had a few drinks and then an overwhelming sense of tiredness came over me, and I knew it was time to sleep. We said our goodnights and agreed to meet at nine for breakfast and then start the journey home.

For the first time in weeks, I felt good, secure now that I was the one back in control. My trajectory could only go back up from here. Back to the top, a happy ending for all. I climbed into the bed and stared at the ceiling. Ok, I think I accepted that my marriage might be irreparable, but I had to try. It could be done, what else was there? And at least I was still alive, I had escaped prison. There was a soft rattle on the door. I had left it unlocked, call it intuition. I turned out the light and the door opened. I could make out the silhouette of the naked woman in the Wellington boots. We knew this would be our last time together like this. She felt small and warm nestling into me under the duvet. We said nothing and within seconds both of us had drifted off into a deep sleep. A final night of tranquillity before it all came to an end. Our last night on this earth.

(Speech written by Tommy Birkby at his father Reginald Birkby's funeral. Widnes Road Church, Liverpool, July 1995)

When I look out at the size of the congregation gathered here, it makes me feel proud of what my father achieved during his life. Most of you will remember him as the local shopkeeper when he ran Birkby and Son from 1948 until he retired in 1987. It is hard to believe that he was only 29 when he took the shop on from the previous owner. We all know he made a success of it and was loved and respected by the local community.

My dad met my mum Mazie in 1950 and I came along a few years later. He always wanted me to take over the shop when he called it a day but even though I did it for a few years, I could not find the enthusiasm that he had. I think my dad was born to be a shopkeeper. He liked people, did not suffer fools and was just the best father ever.

Of course, he could be a tough character when he needed to be. You cannot run a local store and not be able to stand up for yourself. I remember how the locals all rallied around when he was beaten up by some shoplifters with Scottish accents in 1979. We all thought he would die, but typical dad, within three months he was back behind the counter. He never took to a Scottish accent after that,

Kilted robbers he would call them. But I think he was just kidding. How could he be serious when the love of his life, my mum, Mazie was born in Greenock. He used to call her his wee Scotch hen. Mum passed away a few years back and dad was never the same. More than 40 years of the most perfect marriage ever.

Well, Reginald has gone to join Mazie now and I know she will be waiting at the gates for him. An amazing father, a lovely man and our shopkeeper. God bless him.

CHAPTER NINE:
A LEAP INTO
ANOTHER WORLD

(2014)

That is the trouble with being given a fresh start in life. It only remains fresh for a few minutes and then the old problems come back to haunt you. Not that I would have called Roni a problem, a fucking fruit loop maybe, but no, never a problem. I had slept well. Does the condemned man have a peaceful night before he goes to the gallows? I doubt it but then at that point, 7:38 in the morning, I did not realise I was back on death row. By 7:39 I did. That was when I stretched my arm under the duvet in the still dark room to find Roni. She was so slight that sometimes you could lose her in the bed only to discover this little warm ball curled up a few inches away. But it was not human flesh my hand found, it was cold plastic. I shot up out of the bed and grabbed the light switch. There it was, staring back at me in the very space Roni should have been. The black suitcase. I did not even need to look, I knew the money would still be in it.

A cold sweat ran down my forehead as I quickly dressed. I battered on the door to Roni's room but there was no reply. *Oh my god, what has she done and where the fuck is, she?*

I charged on to Charlie's room and rattled the door so hard I am sure I woke the whole hotel up. I could see the light going on and the sound of The Suit scrambling out of his bed in a panic. 'Fuck sake Matt, what the hell is up? I was having a lie in; did you need to bang the bloody door so hard? You damn near gave me a heart attack. What the fuck is…'

'Shut up Charlie. Stop talking and listen. Have you seen Roni, what the hell has she done?' The Suit did shut up when he saw the shock etched in my face.'

'No, I have not seen her Matt. We spoke last night before she went to bed and that was it. What is wrong?' I went in and sat down on his bed before burying my face in my hands. I wanted to weep, scream, punch a hole in the wall, but I just sat there.

'I am finished, Charlie. She must have gone back and

taken the money from him. I dread to think how she got it. Oh god please don't tell me she harmed him. I am done for Charlie, she has gone too far this time.'

'What! What do you mean you have the money back?' The Suit looked as stricken as me.

'Exactly what I fucking said Charlie, I woke to find the case with the 250k back in my room. Oh God in heaven, what has the crazy fucking bitch done this time?' It was maybe a good job that The Suit came and put his arm around me as I think I was about to burst into tears. That would have been embarrassing. I would make a crap gangster, blubbing my eyes out like a big baby.

'Matt, I have something to tell you.' I could read by the tone of his voice that things might not be as bad as they seemed. I looked up in desperation more than hope.

'What, don't tell me you are Roni's long-lost sister, but you had a sex change.'

'You never murdered Birkby, Matt, there was never a reason to be blackmailed. The case was forgotten about years ago.' I was stunned. I looked up at the big man standing over me. He looked ashamed.

'How do you know and when did you find out?' He sat down on the bed beside me.

'I knew before you went to give Kingston the money Matt. I am sorry, really sorry. I don't know why I did not tell you. Maybe I was enjoying this whole thing too much.' I stood up, I should have been angry, but I wasn't. I suppose if I had been honest, I would have admitted that I had enjoyed the whole thing as well. Don't get me wrong, I was desperate for it all to end but it had been an adrenalin rush.

'You mean, you were scared that if I found out it was all a scam then you might not have been able to take me for the 100k I fucking paid you.' He shook his head in sad agreement.

'Yes Matt, that as well. I will pay it back. We will call it quits. It was her, Roni, she knew I was lying and told me last night that I had to tell you, or she would kill me.'

'Kill you?'

'Yes Matt, and the worrying thing is, I think she meant it. That little woman is a fucking mental case.'

It was those last words that Charlie spoke that suddenly brought us back to reality. Where the hell was she and how had she retrieved the money? Maybe she had just simply gone back to see Kingston, told him she knew Birkby had not died and then took the money off him. And yet, that did not seem plausible. Somehow, I knew that if the

two of them had been back in that room together then only
one would be walking out alive. One thing I understood for
sure, I had slept the night with Roni, not Tobi Kingston.
Anyway, if he had tried to share my bed, the fucking thing
would have collapsed into the floor.

We decided to go and search for her. The Suit would
check outside in case she had gone for a walk to buy new
Wellingtons. I would search the restaurant as well as get
a key for her room from the reception. There was no sign
of her in the hotel foyer or canteen, not that I expected
there to be. Somehow the thought of Roni sitting in a hotel
restaurant on her own seemed unlikely. It would be full of
early morning couples and businessmen all staring at Roni
in her Flowery Wellington's. The reception would not give
me a key to her room even though I had paid for it. They did
agree to send someone up with me to check if she was still
sleeping. The place was empty, even the bed had been made.

I went back to my own room to pack. There was
nothing else for it, we would have to drive around Liverpool
and see if we could find her. Maybe check the train station
or the bus station. Even that felt like a waste of time as she
never had more than a few pounds of loose change in her
purse. I started to pull my things together into my now travel

worn case when The Suit came bursting into the room. He was flushed and breathing hard. Charlie was definitely not Olympic material, Sumo wrestling maybe but not the 100 meters or high jump. 'For fuck sake Charlie, slow down. Please tell me you have found her?'

Found who? Oh her, Roni. No, I have not found your girlfriend, Matt but I have found something else, and it is not good.' *Here we go again*, I thought. *Why does this guy never get to the point?*

'She is not my…oh for fuck sake, who cares. What have you found, what have you found?'

'I have found that we have a bigger problem than we first thought Matt, a much bigger problem. In terms of size, let us just say a gargantuan problem.' I sighed and waited. You must all know the score by now. Let him ramble on and eventually, he will get to the point.

'I went to look outside Matt, went to look around the hotel. I found the square root of nothing, zilch. She is gone Matt, gone.'

'I fucking know she has gone, Charlie. That is the reason we are running around like idiots looking for her. Bloody hell man, what is up with you? Can you please stop wasting time stating the obvious? We need to find her quickly, before she does any more damage.

'No not her, not Roni. It is not your fucking girlfriend I am talking about. The fucking car has gone. It is no longer in the car park where you left it last night.'

I turned around in a blind panic to check the side of my bag for the keys. It is an odd human trait that even when we know for absolute certain that something has happened, we still need to look and convince ourselves. But incredibly the keys were still in the bag. No, I am just kidding, they were missing as well. And then my eyes noticed it. *How on earth had I missed it?* I suppose the shock at finding the suitcase in the bed had got to me. I really would make a crap James Bond. In this situation, he would be all control and witty comments. I was close to tears and the only words I could utter were, 'Oh Christ, it's a note from Roni, what the fuck now?'

'What does it say, what does it say?' It was comforting to hear the panic in The Suit's voice, he was no 007 either. I wondered why he was so concerned, this was my problem now, not his.

'Calm down Charlie, give me a fucking chance. Anyway, why are you bothered, you can just walk away from all this.'

'No, I fucking can't Matt, no I fucking can't. I am done

for.'

'What on earth are you talking about Charlie, done for? Why are you done for?'

'Its that crazy fucking girlfriend of yours Matt. The fucking car is hired in my name, she will wreck it for certain. She is madder than a bunch of frogs in a supermarket. That car probably costs 40k, they will charge me the excess. It is 2 grand and now I am not getting paid anymore by you, then I am broke.' I looked at him incredulously, I really wanted to laugh and cry at the same time. This guy was a crazy as Roni, I could not help feeling sorry for him. He was just like a big kid.

'Charlie, whatever happens to the car, I will pay for it. And you know what? Even though you put me through hell by not telling me about Birkby. I am going to let you keep the 100k I already transferred to you. We have far more to worry about than that. We need to find Roni.' He smiled, almost like a child being complimented. I unfolded the note and read the words out loud.

Matt. It is time for you to know the truth. You are no murderer, you never were. Let Mr. Suit explain to you when you meet him this morning. Please do not be angry with him, he is a good guy at heart and thinks the world of you.

He is just immature, that is a good thing to be in a world full of shitheads.

Kingston is dead. I tried to make it look like suicide but even if they are suspicious, it is me they will come looking for. Trust me, Matt, he deserved to die. It was nothing to do with the blackmail. This was personal between me and him.

I never met any decent men in my life, they were all dickheads, every one of them. Except for you Matt. You always tried to look after me, even now. But, I am so glad we never stuck together. We are too different. I would have brought you down to my level and you deserve so much more. I did love you though and if I am honest, I still do.

You need to go back to your normal life now Matt, sort things out with your wife. Get back to playing golf or whatever you rich guys do. Please do not try and find me, you will understand why in a day or two. Tell The Suit not to worry about the hire car, I might not have a license, but I can drive.

P.S. You really do make a crap gangster Matt, far too much of a wimp. xxx

I folded the note and placed it into my pocket before burying my head in my hands. I thought back to yesterday, when she had got out of the car to walk. Roni had been fumbling about in the back of the boot. It was the gun, *the crazy cow had taken the gun and gone back*. My feeling of euphoria and freedom had lasted exactly one night.

The Suit looked at me, waiting for instructions. He was back on my payroll now that I had let him keep the 100k. 'What shall we do Matt?' I had this picture of Roni in my head. Maybe I had lost everything, but I was damned if I was going to lose her as well.

'We need to hire another car. Get it delivered to the hotel, use a different company though, in case they ask what happened to the Jaguar. We have no time to lose Charlie. We need to catch up with her before she gets there.'

'Wow, it will take about twelve hours to get to Bendrennon, Matt. That is a long drive for one person to do.'

'We are not going as far as Bendrennon Charlie, nowhere near as far.' He looked confused but maybe he was finally learning that it was better to shut up and just go along with the ride.

Roni knew she had to get rid of the gun before reaching her final destination. She did not care if it was linked to her and the murder of Tobi Kingston. It was the fact that they would trace it to Charles Cameron Ilderton and eventually Matt might be involved. There was no time to take a major detour off the motorway, it would have to be somewhere near.

The sound of cars and trucks could still be heard rumbling along the M6 as the little woman stood on the moorland. She had taken the exit from the motorway and then followed a track towards what looked like a small lake. It had obviously been dug out by hand many years ago and having been abandoned it was now full of water. Maybe it was an old quarry or overflow to stop the stream that fed it from bursting its banks? The place was not ideal but needs must, she had no time to lose. This would have to do. Roni filled the plastic bag with loose rocks and hurled it out towards the middle of the pool. The small bundle crashed into the water and seemed to float for a few seconds before sinking into the depths. Within minutes she was back in the Jaguar and re-joining the motorway from the slip road. It was only then that she heard the siren and turned to see the Police car easing its way up beside her in the middle lane.

Cameron Jolley had driven this stretch of the motorway so many times before he could probably close his eyes and let the Police car drive itself to Carlisle. His colleague PC George Troutbeck was almost asleep beside him. 'Only an hour until the shift is finished George old chap. Shall we pull into Southwaite services and cadge a coffee?'

'Yes, I could murder a sausage roll as well. Where the fuck are all the lawbreakers today? I am bored shitless.' Cameron was not listening though. He had the Police car in the middle lane, doing just under seventy and was staring at the Jaguar they were slowly edging past. The lady behind the wheel was focused on the road ahead, concentrating or maybe lost in her own thoughts. She looked small inside the large car.

'Bloody hell. That is that Bettina Jesmond.'

'Bettina fucking who?' George had shot up in his seat. He was expecting to hear that his colleague had spotted a well-known criminal.

'Bettina, that cute little woman who was with Charlie. You remember, we met them at the services yesterday.' George raised his eyebrows and sighed with disappointment.

'Bloody Hell Cameron, I thought we were about to get some excitement. Who cares about some middle-aged woman you fancy?' Cameron slowed the police motor up so that it sat alongside the Jaguar. He flicked the siren on for a few seconds to attract Roni's attention and then both he and George leaned over in their seats and waved like two schoolboys. At first, Roni looked confused and then she spotted who it was and smiled while waving back. A few moments later the police car raced away.

'Can we get that bloody sausage roll now that you have had your flirt with the little old lady, Cameron? I am still bloody starving.'

'Old lady, my arse. I would trade my misses in for her.' George laughed at his colleague.

'Come to think of it, you have a point. I would trade my old lady in for the Jaguar XE she is driving. Nice motor. It is a pity she was not speeding or wanted for something, we could have pulled her over. You could have taken her to dinner, and I could have gone for a joy ride.' Cameron nodded in agreement while laughing.

'I bet she has never broken the law in her life. She looks like one of those hippy types, all flowers, and bangles. She probably sings in the church choir.' They were both laughing now as they gunned the car towards the service area and free sausage rolls.

The new hire company delivered the motor to the hotel within two hours. Yes, once again it was me paying. At this rate, I would soon be broke. I don't think my supposed fortune could afford another week of Roni, The Suit, wrecked cars and corpses. We hammered back onto the M6 as fast as we could without attracting attention. I knew where we needed to go to find Roni. I prayed we would not be too late. It was the words she had said when we had visited Bruce's cave as teenagers. The words we had been reminded off yesterday morning in the motel. Maybe I was wrong, and we would not find her there, but I was sure we would. I also knew what she intended to do.

We could jump together into another world.

If that was her intention, then she would have to do it on her own. Now that I had discovered I was innocent, I wanted my life to start again, not end. What was left for Roni, nothing? She could not go back to Bendrennon, there was nobody to go back for. Maybe I just wanted to say goodbye, see her for one last time. I prayed that we would not be too late.

The Suit said very little, I think even he understood that we were heading towards another tragedy. We approached the sign on the M74 for the Sammington exit. A tiny village without a purpose, lost since being bypassed by the motorway. A scattering of houses, one shop, oh and Bruce's Cave. We flew up the main street, hemmed in by the low hills of the Scottish Borders. The sign for Sammington's main attraction looked worn and tired. A track led to a small car park that displayed a shiny new warning.

Dangerous Path. Absolutely no admittance to Bruce's Cave.

We hardly noticed it, both of us staring at the sole occupant of the car park, the black Jaguar XE. Charlie stopped beside it as I grabbed the door handle to make a quick exit. 'My god, you really do know her. How the hell did you work out that she would end up here?'

'Stay in the car Charlie, I will be back. I hope to god it is with Roni.' The Suit was squinting at the warning sign.

'Be careful Matt, they must have closed the path because it is dangerous.' I was already out of earshot as I leaped over the mesh fencing that had been hastily placed in front of the overgrown little track. I edged around it, keeping close to the sheer rock face that bordered one side. The left-hand part of the path was protected by a rotten wooden fence teetering on the edge of a precipice that dropped at least 100 feet down into a swirling narrow river. The water cascaded over the sharp rocks, driven in torrents by the recent rainfall. The opposite side of the thin cutting was also bounded by a sheer rock face, trapping the angry water into a deluge as it sped south towards the sea. One thing I knew for sure, If Roni had already jumped, she would not have survived. The impact would cause her to be crushed to death before being drowned.

There she was, standing at the very tip of oblivion. Even the rotten wooden fence had given up and now the leap into another world lay open and ready for those willing to jump. The scene looked like the place we had visited as happy teenagers without a care in the world. But like the two of us, it was now careworn with the passage of time. The rocks looked older, covered in damp moss. The trees and bushes that protruded at odd angles across the chasm had been allowed to grow untamed. Broken leaves lay scattered all around as winter moved in to reclaim its territory. The two of us blended in perfectly. The lines etched on our faces matching the scars of time carved into the rocks.

I was standing within a few yards of her, but the swirl of the crashing water down below meant I had to shout to be heard. 'Roni, please stand back. Whatever you have done, it does not have to end like this.' She turned around and looked at me. How long had she been standing there? I knew she had been waiting for me to arrive.

'It is ending this way because that is the way it has to end, Matt.'

'Look, Roni, please, I could get you the best lawyer. I

know you must have killed him, and I know he probably deserved it. You could be out in a few years, restart your life.' She smiled and shook her head.

'Oh God Matt, you never get it do you? I have only one regret in life and shooting that fat shit Kingston, is not it. He was a nobody, he deserved what he got.' I said nothing and waited for her to continue.

'That day we came here, back in 1979. We should have jumped then, made the leap into another world. That was the last time I was happy, everything would have ended perfectly. It was all dark after that. It was never the same.' A gust of wind made her frail body sway slightly, any minute now she could fall. Start the journey she longed for.

'I know Roni. But surely everyone feels like that? Life is exciting when you are young. It is just one big carefree adventure. We all have to grow up, maybe that was the part you could not do.' I was sorry I had said that, but it was too late. I could see she was crying, the tears running down her face, dripping onto the Flowery Wellington boots.

'Please go Matt. I am glad I waited, I wanted to say goodbye. I hope they do not find a link between the two of us. I want you to go back to your life, sort things out. You can be free of guilt now, free from regret about what happened with Birkby.'

'I will never be free from guilt or regret Roni. I will miss you every day and wish I had been brave enough to join you.' I stretched my arm out as she did the same, just enough for our fingers to touch. We stayed that way for a few seconds. I started to move forward, and she pulled her hand away to break the spell.

'No Matt, you have to live. Our time will come. I have enough blood on my hands, I won't have yours as well. I have caused enough carnage for one lifetime. There is nothing left for me here, not even you. Please go now. Don't make this any harder than it already is.' Then she turned back around to gaze into the abyss. My chance had gone. It was time to leave her.

'Goodbye Roni, I love you.' But the words floated unheard to join the water crashing over the rocks. I slowly turned and walked back the way I had come without looking back.

I felt empty, as though a part of me had been left behind with Roni. My feet moved and my brain continued to function but without me, without a soul. Like a computer, it started placing things back in order. Filing my life into set operations to be performed. Get the hire cars back, cut all ties with Charlie, finish my last week with Blackbaron and try to mend things with Cara. Pray to God that there would be no link between me and all that had happened in the last few days. Tobi Kingston was dead, and Roni may already have joined him.

And then her face was staring back at me, everything about her was alive inside my head. She had always been there, it was just that I had refused to admit it. *What the hell was I doing? This was all wrong, I can't run away again.*

I ran to the car with Charlie inside it and opened the boot. Grabbing the case, I flung the passenger door open and threw it onto the seat. 'Charlie, don't talk, I have no time.'

'What is it, Matt?'

'Get both of the cars out of here, back to the hire firm. Even if you have to pay a friend to help you.'

'Ok, Ok Matt. but why, what are you going to…'

'Shut up Charlie, I told you, I have no time. Wait until everything has died down and then go and see Cara. Tell her the truth. Give her the case with the money in it. Do you understand me, Charlie?' But whether he did or not no longer mattered, I was leaping over the metal fence, running, only seconds left.

She was already starting to fall, the merest hint of

forward motion but already there could be no going back. Roni heard my desperate footsteps and even as she started her journey into the next world, she had time to turn and see me. I would not make it to the gap in the wooden fence in time, there was only one way. I ran straight into the rotting remains of the ancient barrier and jumped with every ounce of energy I had left. Our bodies collided and joined as we floated into the air. A tiny fraction of time before we would both be crushed on the watery rocks below. Happy again, the way we had been so many years ago. Together at last as we moved across into another world. One that would be free of guilt, one where we could be with each other always. Young and carefree again, forever joined at the mouth of Bruce's cave.

(Dumfries and Galloway Post. December 2014)

Police have confirmed that the two bodies found within a mile of each other in Clethan Water near Sammington are those of Matt Cunningham and Roni Paterson. Cunningham had been reported as missing more than two months ago while it had only recently come to light that Paterson had not been seen in her home village of Bendrennon in Sutherland for some months. Police have yet to confirm if the two deaths are linked although they have said that both were tragic suicides.

Matt Cunningham was a business celebrity having steered IT firm Blackbaron Technologies through a difficult operating climate during the last ten years. He had only just announced his retirement after 30 years with the company, including the last 7 as head of UK operations. His wife Cara Cunningham spoke highly of her husband stating he was a wonderful partner and father. She did mention that Mr. Cunningham had been suffering from depression during the last few years and had found his upcoming retirement to be a particularly traumatic period in his life.

It had been expected that Mr. Cunningham would receive an OBE in the next honours list for outstanding services to industry. Although he had a reputation for reducing workforce numbers, Mr. Cunningham was the main driving factor in the successful turn-around of Blackbaron in the United Kingdom. The new head of UK operations, Brian Sutherland was quoted as saying, *Matt was one of the hardest working and most honest people I had the good fortune to work beside. He earned his retirement and it is so sad that he did not get to enjoy it.*

Over 1000 people attended Mr. Cunningham's funeral on the outskirts of Glasgow including well-known business figures and minor celebrities.

Roni Paterson was known to have had a troubled past and had suffered throughout her life with alcohol problems. She was buried near her last known abode in Sutherland. Her friend Annie Leatherface McGowan attended with a few others. She spoke highly of Miss Paterson saying, She wiz nabodies fool wiz ur wee Rosie Cheeks. Al fer miss the wee lassie.

(Liverpool Music Scene magazine October 2014)

It has been confirmed that musician Tobi Kingston committed suicide at his flat in Colby Terrace, Liverpool last Friday. Kingston had recently moved from Scotland to look after his ailing mother. He first found fame with the early seventies rock band Drangonesque who he made one album with. It charted at number 85 in the UK chart but the band then faded from the scene.

Kingston made many further attempts to break into the music world after quitting Dragonesque. His other bands included punk outfit, Social Decline, new wave band, Sparkling Leotard, heavy metal band, The Daggers of Babylon, Soft rock group, Secret Kiss, Grunge outfit, Filth, Rave band The Unhappy Tuesdays and X factor failures, Three Fat Men.

CHAPTER TEN:
CURTAIN CALL

(Today)

Have you ever been to the theatre? I mean the real theatre, the one where people are on stage and they act out a play. Of course, you have, even I went once when my wife dragged me along. One of those amateur dramatics' things. To be fair, they are usually pretty good, in a slightly embarrassing way. Ok, let us just assume you have all been to a play at some time and sat there casting a critical eye over the performance. Well, you know the bit at the end? Yes, that part where they come out and introduce each actor, in a kind of order of importance. Then they all join together for one last big bow? You with me so far?

I bet you are wondering, what the fuck is this guy on about? Give me a chance will you, I am getting there. So, you are sitting with the love of your life in the audience at this supposed play, watching the actors come out to take their bow. Now think. Have you ever noticed that the audience response is usually based on how they perceived the character in the play? What I mean is, they applaud if he or she was a good guy and boo if they played a villain. It has nothing to do with how well they performed as actors.

Do you not think that is a bit unfair? I do and you know why? I was standing in the wings with the rest of the characters from our little story and I was as nervous as hell. Maybe I am too competitive, but I will tell you something. I was going to be annoyed if Charlie or Roni got a bigger ovation than me. Bloody hell, it could even be worse, maybe Tobi Kingston would get a bigger hand than I did?

'Ladies and Gentlemen, I hope you have enjoyed our little drama tonight. Now it is time to introduce the main players and I am sure you will give each of them a good round of applause for their sterling effort to entertain us all this evening.' *Oh, Fuck, here goes,* I thought.

'Put your hands together for Mr. Reginald Birkby, the shopkeeper who came back from the dead.' *Can you believe it, some of the audience were on their feet? I mean come on, he hardly had a thing to do in the whole tale other than roll about for a few seconds in a pool of blood. And don't forget, the fucker put me through hell pretending he had died.*

'Our two intrepid policemen, Cameron Jolley, and George Troutbeck. Guardians of our safety on the motorway' *Guardians fuck all. The pair of skiving bastards spent most of their time either eating sausage rolls or trying to chat Roni up. And you guessed it, the bloody audience nearly wet themselves applauding the two lazy sods.*

'Let's hear it for everyone's favourite Pilates lady, Cara Cunningham.' *More enthusiastic applause. This was not looking good. I mean I know she probably deserved it after having to put up with me as her husband, but I had a feeling the clapping was really to get a dig at me.*

'And the man who tried to steal Cara in her moment of crisis, Mr. Eric Carter.' *This was more like it, muted applause and even a few boos from the audience. Poor old Eric, but I was laughing inside. I still chuckle every now and then at the thought of the big baboon standing holding two cups of coffee in the snow after Cara drove off.*

'And please give a big thank you to Annie Leather Face and her friends, Marco Gob Shite, Bennie The Fox, Copper Lamp Bill, Teflon Tony, and Tam Empty Pockets.' *They shuffled on like death warmed up. Well to be fair most of them were dead, just like me. I think you can guess that the audience went crazy for Annie and her associated drinking* buddies. *I work hard all my life and a bunch of alcoholics who never had a job end up with all the applause. I did like the little Kilmarnock gang though. I would have taken them for a beer if I had still been alive. Too late now I suppose.*

'And finally, our three big players.' *Oh fuck, here we go, please like me, please like me.*

'Mr. Charles Cameron Ilderton or The Suit as we know and love him.' *He had hardly taken his first step forward from the side of the stage before the crowd stood up and went fucking crazy, seriously fucking crazy. I mean come on, give me a break. Charlie was a nice guy but bloody hell, he was a conman and not even a good one. He would have done fuck all if I had not paid him. It cost me a 100 grand and you lot are making out he is some sort of superhero. Jeez, there is no accounting for people sometimes.*

'And now we are down to our last two. The main stars of our little tale.' *I was sweating now. You see the problem was, when they asked me to appear in this story, I was supposed to be the main player. The book was supposed to be about me, Roni was to be my co-star. But I had this feeling that by the end I had become the supporting role to our little Kilmarnock bombshell. The compere put the mic up to his mouth, if he said my name first then I had indeed been relegated to second place.*

'Please, Give a big round of applause for the man with the money, Mr. Matt Cunningham.' *To be fair, the audience did give me a great reception. A few boos but mostly cheers. Maybe some of them wanted a job at Blackbaron? Well if they did, they can forget it. I am retired, oh hang on. I forgot, I am fucking dead as well. Retired and dead, great combination.*

'And last but not least, please, a big hand, be upstanding for.' *Oh, fucking get on with it will you.*

'Our heroine, Miss Roni Paterson or should I say, Wee Rosie Cheeks.' *He drew the words out, so they lasted twice as long as they had when he said my name. I seriously thought the audience was going to invade the stage. Good job they held back at the last minute, Roni would have either hit them with a flower pot or shot them. I had to admit, she deserved the ovation, or maybe it was the flowery Wellington boots they were clapping?*

We all came together on the stage for one last bow. Looking at the characters lined up either side made me realise we had all been involved in a bit of a morbid tale. Me, Roni, Tobi, Birkby, and Annie were now all deceased. Even Leather Faces chums were mostly gone. Tam Empty Pockets being the exception, but he was in a care home. They tell me they found 20,000 pounds hidden under the mattress in his flat. That left just the two policemen, Cara, Eric, and Charlie to roam the world of the living for a while longer. I always wondered if Cara and Eric would become an item, but I doubted it. She was far too smart for him. I shouted above the din to her. 'Did you get the case with the money in it from Charlie?'

'What money? He never gave me anything.' I looked at The Suit who was standing next to me. He looked flustered and embarrassed.

'I was going to get it to her Matt, honestly, I was. I just, sort of, forgot.' I shook my head and laughed.

As we took our bow, I could feel Roni's hand pinch my rear. 'Christ Roni, not in front of the theatre, please.' She smiled and silently whispered,

'Oh, for fuck sake Matt, stop moaning. You are just in a bad mood because I got a bigger round of applause than you.' And you know what? She was right and she fully deserved it.

The Path by Richard M Pearson

On a path filled with ghosts and secrets, nobody is safe.

For neurotic Ralph and easy-going Harvey, the trek across the remote, rolling hills of Scotland is a chance to get away from life, an opportunity to rediscover their place in the world. At least that's the plan. But they are two middle-aged, unfit men trying to cross one hundred miles of rugged terrain.

Despite that, they might have had a chance if that was their only problem. Unfortunately, not only are they alcoholics, someone or something is stalking them, watching their every move. Worse, one man carries a terrible secret about why he went on the trip. A secret that will turn a friendly trek into something far darker. It's a safe bet that if either man survives, he will never be the same again.

The Path is the first novel by Richard M Pearson. A gothic ghost story for modern times that builds up an atmosphere of foreboding and fear.

A terrific read. Thoroughly enjoyed this novel. Atmospheric, melancholic, laced with pathos and wry humour. Excellent plot and an intriguing outcome. Strong characterisation, complex and endearing personas, more so for their flaws and imperfections. The poems were also a nice touch. Almost offering a staging post for the author's state of mind as each chapter ends. I can highly recommend The Path, it won't disappoint.

(Available on Amazon)

RICHARD M
PEARSON

THE
PATH

A GHOST STORY?

Deadwater by Richard M Pearson
Who would dare to unlock the secret of Deadwater Mansion?

It is only when you look back at things from the distance of many years that you finally understand why. The problem was we in the village blamed the aristocratic Denham-Granger family for our bad fortune. Everything was their fault according to us but in hindsight, that was more to do with jealousy than reality. We hated them because they had wealth and looked down on us as uneducated peasants.

But the truth was, they were as much victims as we were. No, the real holder of all the power through the years was Deadwater. The grand three-story country mansion cast its shadow over the village and manipulated everything to survive. So, when it realised that time was running out it played the final card, and then dark retribution crawled out of that room to hunt each of its victims down.

Deadwater, A Classic Gothic Ghost Story with a shocking twist.

(Available on Amazon)

FROM THE AUTHOR OF 'THE PATH'

RICHARD M
PEARSON

DEADWATER

WHO CAN FREE THE SECRET OF DEADWATER HOUSE?

61604270R00157

Made in the USA
Columbia, SC
24 June 2019